Strictly Christmas Spirit

Titles in the Spotlight series:
Strictly on Ice
Celebrity SOS: Love Survives
Strictly Christmas Spirit
Keeping Up with the Kershaws

Strictly Christmas Spirit

Helen Buckley

Where heroes are like chocolate – irresistible!

Copyright © 2022 Helen Buckley

Published 2022 by Choc Lit Limited
Penrose House, Crawley Drive, Camberley, Surrey GU15 2AB, UK
www.choc-lit.com

The right of Helen Buckley to be identified as the Author of this Work
has been asserted by her in accordance with the Copyright, Designs and
Patents Act 1988

A CIP catalogue record for this book is available
from the British Library

ISBN 978-1-78189-510-8

Printed and bound in Great Britain
by Clays Ltd, Elcograf S.p.A.

For David, Donovan and Richard
– my everything.

Acknowledgements

Firstly, I'd like to thank Choc Lit for bringing *Strictly Christmas Spirit* to publication, and the wonderful Choc Lit Tasting Panel who gave my festive story the thumbs up – Kate Avetoomyan, Danielle Arch, Siobhan Bray, Chloe Murphy, Liana Vera Saez, Helen Maddison, Bee Master, Alma Hough, Lorna Baker, Lyndsey Gilchrist, Haley Eyre, Honor Gilbert, Debbie Southwell, Carol Orpwood, Deborah Warren, Vanessa Wick, Jo Osborne, Ruth Nägele and Sharon Walsh.

I couldn't write this book without a few very special people in mind. Captains Lee and Jonathan Raggett, Lieutenant Tony Kakande, and Rebecca Cheadle. They were my colleagues when I was a Community Centre Manager for the Salvation Army in London – the job which provided a lot of inspiration for this story.

I will never forget the hours we spent in that tiny office – laughing and fretting and praying and working so hard together, hoping and trying to make a difference in the lives of the people who walked through the door each day. The experience has always stayed with me, and therefore so have you all. Thank you for the generous words, the support and the hazelnut lattes (Lee!)

Thank you to my group of readers and friends who help me so much with feedback, advice and supportive words – Helen Bowen, Amanda Gee, Sarah Bickerton, Rachel Raine, Danielle Desanges and Mum, who reads everything I write.

Thank you to my sister-in-law and probation expert Laura Buckley, who kindly took the time to answer all my questions about community service so the story of Blake isn't wholly and completely inaccurate.

Finally, thank you to my husband David. Without your support and encouragement and wisdom, I would be lost. You are, and will always be, my leading man.

Prologue

→ EMILY ←

The studio went dark and all Emily could hear was the thudding of her heart, the rushing of blood in her ears as her adrenaline kicked in. She paused at the top of the steps to wait for her cue, one sizzling spotlight trained on her, the heat of the light caressing her- shoulders. She looked over at where Kian was standing in the centre of the dancefloor, his head bowed and shoulders tense. They had practised the steps over and over again, but she was worried about his stage fright. She had tried to reassure Kian that he would be fine, but the footballer's almost hysterical nerves as they warmed up hadn't exactly filled her with confidence.

There was a brief silence, and to Emily it seemed to stretch on for minutes, but it was really only a few seconds before the announcement came.

'Dancing the salsa, Kian Roberts and Emily Williams!'

The music started, the punchy opening sequence of 'Conga', and Emily began the routine, swaying her hips, but she could see that Kian was already off the rhythm. *Damn*, she cursed inwardly. She sashayed quickly up to him, putting a hand on his chest, pulling him to her as she tried to get him back on time.

Despite his obvious efforts and multiple rehearsals, Kian's footballer's muscles just couldn't master the smooth undulations of the sexy salsa. He was slow on the

1

turns, heavy on his feet and stiff in his hips; all of this was made worse by his seeming inability to count the beat.

Emily gritted her teeth behind her brightly lipsticked smile. Normally, she would enjoy this song, energised by the vibrant piano interspersed with lively trumpets and an infectious rhythm, but all she could think about was how much she didn't want to leave the competition too early. Kian was already a millionaire, but this was her career and livelihood he was messing up if they got voted off too soon. She was twenty years old and being on *Strictly Dancing with Celebs* was the greatest opportunity she could ever have. She wanted to get the most out of it.

The audience clapped along, whooping enthusiastically. She tried to feed off their energy, to focus on the buzz of being on TV's greatest dancing show. She swished her hips, her sparkling gold skirt swirling around her thighs, every sequin reflecting the bright yellow lights that beamed around the studio. But, try as she might, all the hip swaying, sensual strutting and complex footwork in the world couldn't stop Kian from looking like a fish out of water.

The footballer gave her a desperate look, perspiration beading on his forehead. He was a gorgeous young man, somehow managing to pull off a gold glittery jacket with aplomb, but he just couldn't get the steps right. Emily smiled reassuringly at him, clutching his hand, but the band seemed to speed up, the bright jangling of the song almost manic, and still they lagged behind.

Emily knew the judges would be harsh. She just hoped the public might be kinder.

After all, this was *Strictly Dancing with Celebs*; her dream come true, all her Christmases come at once. Surely it couldn't all be over already, could it?

Chapter One

✦ BLAKE ✦

Blake wielded his remote at the TV as the opening sequence for *Strictly Dancing with Celebs* burst onto his screen.

'Load of rubbish,' he muttered darkly and changed the channel, only to find a Christmas advert – in September! The voiceover simpered about family and togetherness, and Blake snorted with exasperation and threw the remote at the TV, where it bounced off harmlessly.

He stomped over to the bar and poured himself a glass of vodka, swirling it around, creating a mini whirlpool at its centre. He stared at it for a moment, imagining a tiny version of himself drowning in it, then he tilted the glass back with one quick motion and swallowed it all in one gulp. He winced at the rawness in his throat and poured some more, clumsily tilting the vodka bottle and sloshing the liquid over the sides, where it pooled onto the coffee table.

He returned to his seat and leaned over the table, sifting through the pile of papers in front of him. He took a sheet and picked it up, holding it delicately by the edges, then set his lighter to it. The flame trembled in unison with the shakiness of his hand, until he finally managed to make the lighter meet the paper where the flame licked at it hungrily, the edges of the page furling away from the heat. He didn't let go until the flame had eaten up the words *Decree Absolute*, and only dropped the page into the empty ice bucket when the heat seared at his fingers.

He picked up the next page and did the same, and then again, filling the bucket with smoking ashes. He poured himself another drink and threw it down his throat, the vodka running down his chin. His hands left ashen smudges around the glass and the bottle, but he couldn't feel the burning in his fingertips anymore, which he took to be a good sign.

He tilted the bottle of vodka once more, but it was already empty. He glared at it, raised his arm and threw it across the room. It landed with a thud on the sofa. He clenched his fists, feeling a surge of fury at the empty bottle and the empty promises it contained. He wrapped his fingers around his glass and threw it as hard as he could against the wall, feeling a jolt of pleasure as it cracked and spattered glass fragments everywhere. He got up and stood over the remains of the glass, grinding the fragments into the carpet with the toe of his shoe. In a pristine hotel room filled with luxurious soft furnishings, the shattered glass was the one thing that seemed to suit him. He felt broken and jagged; a jumble of mistakes and sharp edges that nobody should get too close to, lest they snag something on him.

He swung round unsteadily and grabbed a chair by the legs. *This was going to be fun.*

December

✦ EMILY ✦

'Emily, the sandwiches have run out!'

'Emily, do you have food bank vouchers?'

Emily whipped round as several voices called her name at once. The community centre was bustling with people, and she tried not to bump into anyone or spill her coffee as she hurried from one thing to the next. She grabbed her food bank voucher booklet from her pocket, pointed Fernando in the direction of the extra sandwiches, took a sip of lukewarm coffee, and kept smiling even though her head was spinning with other people's demands. As she scurried and hopped from one person to another, she felt like she was doing a quickstep, dancing to the beat of everyone else's needs but her own.

Despite the freezing wind that blew in regularly from the entrance, she was sticky with sweat, both from the busyness of the day and the body heat of all the people crowding in. One of the other local drop-in centres was closed for staff training so Emily's centre had an extra influx of people that morning. *At least the other centre had the courtesy to let me know*, thought Emily gratefully, thankful for the extra portions of porridge that Fernando had cooked up in preparation.

She was already on her third cup of coffee and it was only 9 a.m. She could feel the caffeine jangling in her veins, giving her a slight head buzz and a jittery feeling in her legs. She needed that extra energy after Rocky had kept her up all night, singing joyfully in his screechy little voice. *The damn parrot*, she cursed, as she stifled a yawn and greeted the next person to come in through the door.

'Morning,' she said, warmly. 'It's Pavel, isn't it?'

The young man's surly expression was softened by a hopeful smile. *What a difference, it made*, Emily thought, *to remember someone's name and give them a decent welcome, especially at this time of year*. 'Please come in and help yourself to some food and a hot drink,' she said. Pavel nodded, hefting his large backpack over his shoulder, and walked into the hall, eager to escape the bitter cold outside.

Emily looked around proudly at the Christmas lights they had put up yesterday, which glowed merrily around the centre, their twinkling colours softening the harsh white gleam of the fluorescent strip lighting. The shimmering foil decorations swung from the ceiling, blown about by the breeze from the door. They were tacky and old-fashioned, but Emily finally felt like Christmas was on the way, and she hoped the decorations would bring a bit of festive cheer to people who came in today; people who were homeless or struggling or simply lonely.

There was just the Christmas tree left to decorate, and she was excited to get it out of storage, not caring that it was made of plastic and needed dusting. It just wouldn't feel properly Christmassy until the tree was up, at least not to her. She was planning to make the most of her afternoon by decorating it, especially as it was a Friday – it would be a nice way to end the week.

Lizzie, her colleague and the centre keyworker, leaned out of the door to the office, calling her name and interrupting her wishful thoughts of Christmas tree decorating. 'Emily! There's a phone call for you.'

Emily looked around with a sigh. She hated taking calls while the centre was so busy. Something would nearly always happen while she was shut in the office, and she needed to be out among the drop-in clients and volunteers, making sure everything was running smoothly. As much as she trusted her volunteer team, she knew it wasn't fair to leave them in charge of everything. That was her job, and it was a heavy responsibility – one that she often felt she couldn't put down even for a few moments.

'Who is it?' she asked, slightly exasperated.

'Rowan,' Lizzie said, chuckling at her reaction as Emily groaned out loud, smacking her palm on her forehead. The last person she wanted to talk to right now was her area manager.

Lizzie pushed her glasses up her nose, from where they were perpetually falling down. 'He's waiting.' She indicated the phone.

Emily nodded resignedly. 'Darren, can you take over at the door please?' she called to one of her volunteers. Darren nodded happily, always eager to help. He was a student at a nearby university and she loved his enthusiasm.

Emily shut the office door as Lizzie left her to her phone call. The office was small, with two narrow desks, a few chairs and numerous post-it notes littering the wall, covered with Emily's handwriting that even she herself couldn't read. A coat rack in the corner overflowed with jackets and took up valuable space. While Lizzie's desk was fairly spartan, Emily's desk overflowed with a jumbled pile of papers and personal effects. There were files piled high, scrawled notes bunched up underneath the keyboard to remind her of tasks she could never get round to, and a number of old coffee mugs, growing various species of mould. Emily had plonked a tiny Christmas tree on top of it all; it stood jauntily, its cheery brightness undeterred by the refuse surrounding it.

Emily sat down at her desk, sweeping her enormous woollen scarf off her chair, and steeled herself. Rowan was a good area manager, but she and him had never seen eye-to-eye about how best to run the centre. He was an expert in fundraising and marketing, obsessed with social media, whereas Emily was much more interested in the people visiting them for help, and she wasn't brilliant at paperwork, or reports, or budgets. She knew the charity needed Rowan's marketing savvy to make sure the donations kept coming, but his inability to see her side of things frustrated her terribly.

'Rowan,' she said, picking up the handset. 'How are things?'

'Excellent!' he boomed jovially down the phone, making her ear ring.

'You've had good news about the funding application?' she asked hopefully. The centre was operating on a shoe string, and was desperately in need of more funding for staff and projects. She was counting on Rowan's expertise to help them get it.

'Even better!' he said excitedly. 'I have brilliant news for you, Emily. You're getting a new volunteer for a week or so in the run-up to Christmas.'

Emily frowned, grateful it wasn't a video call so Rowan couldn't see her irritated expression. She was in charge of volunteer recruitment and training for the centre, not Rowan. 'Um, okay ...' she said, trying to pick her words carefully. 'Is it someone who applied directly to you?' she asked, knowing that interns sometimes sent their CVs straight to head office.

'Nope, get this. You're not going to believe it.' Rowan paused for dramatic effect and she shifted impatiently in her chair, wanting to tell him to hurry up and let her get back to work. 'You're getting none other than Blake Harris for his community service stint.' She didn't reply. 'You know? The actor Blake Harris?' he prompted.

Emily's heart sank. 'I know of him,' she mumbled unenthusiastically. 'Wouldn't he be better off going to one of the larger centres?' she said, hoping Rowan could reassign him. The last thing she wanted was to be babysitting a petulant actor with a penchant for trashing hotel rooms. She was already so busy and working late every evening. She simply didn't have time to supervise a film star who was forced to volunteer by a judge.

'He's going to your centre,' Rowan said firmly. 'I'm sure we can use it to our advantage when he's finished, maybe get some good photos of him with the clients to use in fundraising materials, perhaps an endorsement from him, maybe even a donation?' He was burbling and sounded completely star-struck, and Emily felt a pang of irritation that he was imposing this on her. She knew that the charity's head office had worked with probation on community service orders before, but never someone as high profile as Blake Harris. Despite his reputation hanging by a thread, and his last few films bombing both with critics and the public, Blake was still seen as hot property – *and* he was the son of Hollywood royalty too.

Emily bit her lip. She knew Rowan was right; having someone like Blake Harris at the centre could present some useful opportunities. 'When does he start?' she asked, resigning herself to Rowan's plan.

'He'll be with you Monday morning at 9 a.m. for a quick orientation, then he'll start his hours on Tuesday and stay till the following Thursday,' Rowan replied.

Emily sighed and rubbed her forehead hard in frustration at the lack of notice. *Typical Rowan behaviour.* 'Fine,' she said curtly. 'We'll be ready for Mr Harris on Monday.'

'Great, I'll email you everything you need,' Rowan said, sounding pleased.

She hung up and thought sadly of the afternoon she had set aside for decorating the Christmas tree, which would now be taken up by paperwork to prepare for Blake's arrival. She rolled her shoulders to ease the tension that had crept up on her.

'Emily!' she heard her name being called with a hurried knock. Darren poked his head around the door, looking flustered and wide-eyed with panic. 'Come quick, there's been an argument over the sandwiches!'

Emily got to her feet and took a breath, ready to intervene and restore calm. She would have to prepare for Blake's arrival later. Right now, Mr Hollywood was at the bottom of her to-do list.

✦ BLAKE ✦

Blake tapped his foot impatiently while his agent, Alice Crawford, scowled as she clicked through her emails. She shot him a stern look and he stopped tapping, but he was irritated at how long it was taking her to respond to his simple question. Alice carried on scrolling. 'Here it is,' she murmured, finally finding the email she had been looking for.

'Tell me my agent extraordinaire hasn't let me down,' he said hopefully.

Alice raked her fingers through her platinum-blonde pixie cut and couldn't keep a grimace from twisting over her scarlet lips. 'I'm sorry to have to tell you Blake, but both of the offers have been rescinded.'

Blake dropped his head into his hands with a groan. 'What?! Because of some piddly little hotel room incident?'

She shook her head and drummed her nails on the desk, her gun-metal nail varnish gleaming in the office lights. 'To be fair, Scorsese was on the fence about you in the first place, and the part wasn't a guarantee.'

'What about Spielberg?' he muttered.

'The role was for someone clean-cut. They wanted someone a bit more …' she hesitated.

'Bland? Boring?' Blake interjected sarcastically.

Alice cleared her throat. 'Family-friendly,' she said finally.

Blake snorted derisively. 'So, who did they choose over me then?'

'Eddie Redmayne.'

'Bloody hell!' Blake threw up his hands, feeling a surge of irritation at losing out on work he was not only interested in, but also really needed, especially as the last two projects he'd been involved in had been disastrous, not to mention his latest weddings and divorces being extremely costly. 'What am I paying you for, Alice?' he snapped at her, ignoring the frown that flitted across her face at his petulant tone.

She put her hands on the desk and leaned forward. 'Listen, Blake. You know I love you, but you need to sort out this mess and get your head back in the game,' she said firmly.

He leaned back in his chair, tipping it onto the two back legs, and folded his arms. He gave her his moodiest look, knowing that she was right and wishing she wasn't.

'Since you split up from Anita, you've been all over the place. We had the terrible reviews for *The Brave and Wild*, that car-crash TV interview and then the hotel incident to top it all off,' she continued.

Blake winced at the mention of his last film, the reviews for which had been universally bad. He had known during filming that he'd only been going through the motions, paralysed by his addictions, blank behind the eyes, sleepwalking through every scene, the thought of his next drink going round and round his head. He wasn't surprised the critics had panned his performance, not that he had cared much at the time. It was difficult to care when painkillers and alcohol had cauterised his brain. He knew he shouldn't have done the interview with Holden Banks but he had gone ahead, despite Alice's pleas, stubbornly refusing to believe it was a bad idea. He had cursed and slurred and stumbled through it, rambling and talking nonsense. He could barely remember doing it, but if he needed a reminder the footage was still clocking up views on YouTube for all the world to see.

'I know rehab was hard,' Alice said, as he sat in sullen silence. 'You've done marvellously with your recovery. But now it's time to stop acting like a brat – you need to complete your community order, act like you're sorry and get some good headlines for once.'

Blake stared at her without blinking, and Alice met his gaze with a cool smile. She had been his agent for a long time and was the only one who ever spoke to him as frankly as this. He'd told her to piss off so many times, but she knew he never meant it. He'd sacked and lost a lot of publicists, PAs, drivers, housekeepers, all sorts of staff over the years, who could never quite keep up with his chameleonic moods and alcohol-induced tempers, but Alice was the only one who stuck with him through it all. Despite his annoyance, despite feeling totally fed up, his small sense of gratitude for Alice shone a golden light into his current black mood.

Blake cleared his throat and sat up straight. 'Maybe I could get married again?' he offered, trying to be helpful. 'That always gets some nice headlines.'

Alice looked down at her desk. 'I think three divorces has undone that good coverage, Blake,' she murmured.

He heaved a sigh. 'All right, fine. So, I have to do this community service. At least can we make sure my good work is noted? Get some photos of me in the press?'

Alice nodded slowly. 'Yes, we can do that. We probably won't be able to have cameras inside the project – you know, safeguarding, privacy, etc – but we can get some of you going in, some quotes about how well you're doing, that sort of thing.'

'Yeah!' Blake exclaimed, his enthusiasm flaring a little at the idea of being portrayed as someone kind and giving and generous, especially so near to Christmas. 'It'll show me in a positive light for once, you know, helping out all those—' he paused, trying to remember who he was going to be helping '—orphans?' He took a guess.

Alice shook her head with a slight smile. 'It's a community centre, so older people, the homeless, vulnerable people in need, that sort of thing,' she explained.

Blake made a face. 'Great. It'd be good if we can get some shots of me serving soup to the poor sods, if that's possible.'

Alice grinned. 'I'll see what we can do.'

Blake leaned back and put his hands behind his head. If he was going to have to spend almost two weeks of his precious time helping smelly vagrants, he might as well get something out of it for himself.

Chapter Two

Emily was putting the final touches to her arts and crafts plan when the doorbell rang, the shrillness breaking through the calm silence that was so rare in the centre. They were closed that Monday morning, making it an ideal time for her latest "volunteer" to arrive for an orientation. She clasped the folder of notes and safeguarding briefings that she had prepared and checked the intercom. As expected, it was Blake Harris. She had seen his storm-grey eyes and defined cheekbones on the big screen, but now his instantly recognisable features were peering into her intercom.

'I'll be right there!' She hurried to the door, jamming her hand on the button to open it. The automatic door swung open slowly to reveal Blake lounging with his hands in his pockets and a nonchalant smile on his face. His six-foot-three-inch frame was clad all in black, with his raven hair swept back off his face, a smattering of dark stubble grazing his chin. His skin was a healthy tanned colour, which Emily assumed he had year-round thanks to his second home in LA.

She stepped back from the doorway. 'Come in, Mr Harris.'

He walked in, extending his hand to her. She shook it firmly, still not quite able to believe it was Blake in the flesh. She had met celebrities before, in her previous line of work, but no one near as famous as Blake. And no one near as handsome, not that his looks were important for this new role the judge had assigned him.

'Nice to meet you, Emma,' he said politely. His mouth curved upwards in a smile, but his tone was flatly unenthusiastic and his eyes remained gloomy.

'Oh, actually my name is—' she made to correct him, but before she could finish, he interrupted her.

'I hope you don't mind, but I told my driver to park outside.' He indicated a large SUV with blacked-out windows.

'It's no parking down here,' she said, pointing to the red lines at the kerb. 'You'll get a ticket within minutes.'

'That's okay.' He gave an unbothered shrug. 'It's easier to have the car close by.'

'Right, well, it's your choice,' she said, a little surprised at his non-compliance with parking restrictions but then remembering that he could no doubt easily afford the fines. 'Would you like to follow me to the office?'

Blake walked behind her as she showed him to her desk and invited him to sit down. 'Can I get you a coffee or tea?' she asked.

He rested one ankle on his knee. 'Coffee, black and sweet,' he said, with no attempt at basic courtesy. He looked around him with an unimpressed expression whilst Emily went to fetch his coffee. She stirred the granules in briskly, banging the spoon down on the kitchen counter, irked at Blake's lack of basic manners. She headed back to the office and handed him the mug, not expecting him to thank her for her efforts.

'Right,' she said, sitting down at her desk. 'Let's—'

'Is this instant?' he interjected, sniffing his mug suspiciously.

'Yes,' she said, watching as he carefully placed his mug on the desk and gently pushed it away from him with the tip of his middle finger.

'I only drink freshly ground, ideally Ethiopian,' he explained, noting her observing him.

Emily cleared her throat, which was tight with annoyance. 'We don't have that here,' she said brusquely, rifling the papers in her hands, keen to get started so she could get on with her other work for the day.

Blake raised an eyebrow and let out a small sigh.

'Welcome to the community centre,' she said, ignoring his obvious disdain and trying to put aside her preconceptions and be as professional and courteous as possible to this Hollywood brat. 'Thank you for your interest in helping us out for the next couple of weeks.'

Blake snorted incredulously. 'Under duress,' he said glumly, his slate-grey eyes dark and ponderous like gathering clouds before a storm.

Emily coughed uncomfortably. She hadn't really wanted to mention the court case. She felt like it was none of her business and she just wanted to get the next two weeks over and done with. She ignored his comment and carried on. 'We do a number of activities here at the centre, mainly serving people who are homeless, or in difficult housing situations, plus older, lonely and vulnerable people, and those with physical and mental ill-health.'

'So, some of them are, you know … nutso?' He gave her an amused smile, revealing the whitest teeth Emily had ever seen.

'We prefer not to use such derogatory terms,' she snipped at his glib comment, and his grin fell away. She tried to shake off her growing unease at his attitude and cleared her throat. 'We have a couple of drop-in sessions a week offering hot meals and sandwiches, plus an arts and crafts class, and I lead a dance session,' she said, proud of the variety of activities they put on with such a shoestring budget. 'We also run a temporary weekly night shelter in winter, in partnership with other local homeless projects.'

She paused and Blake nodded, his face blank and uninterested. 'I've printed off some notes for you, about our activities and the type of people we help.' She offered him the binder she had prepared for him. He reached out and took it, flicking through the pages quickly.

'Very organised, Emma,' he noted.

'Emily,' she corrected him.

'Right,' he said. 'Well, I'm sure this will make great reading for later.' She thought she detected an edge of sarcasm in his voice and hoped she was mistaken.

'While you're here, your main role will be helping out with the activities,' Emily explained. 'You know, chatting to people, cooking and serving food for the drop-ins, cleaning up afterwards, that kind of thing.'

He raised an eyebrow and coolly met her gaze without offering a response.

'I, erm, I hope that you'll find it to be a rewarding experience,' she stammered, unnerved by his lack of interest.

'I'm sure it'll be wonderful,' he said flatly.

Given his distinct lack of enthusiasm so far, she was taken aback when he suddenly leaned forward, his expression brightening as though he had flicked a switch to access his famous charm that made him so appealing on the big screen. 'I appreciate the opportunity to be here and contribute,' he said. 'And I do hope it'll be okay if I can get some photos of the experience to—' he paused, as if searching for the right words '—shine a light on your good works,' he said eventually.

And show off your nice side to the public as well I bet, Emily thought, although she didn't say it aloud as she stared at him.

'Listen, Mr Harris,' she began in her best managerial voice, the one she put on when she was dealing with complaints or fights, or volunteers who just wouldn't do what they were told. 'Some of our clients are extremely vulnerable, or from very difficult home situations. I don't think they'd be comfortable being in promotional photographs for press or social media.' She remembered that Rowan had suggested the exact same thing, but she knew her service users and doubted they would be happy to be photographed, regardless of whether or not it could be a good fundraising opportunity for the centre. Emily didn't trust the press, and she tried to keep journalists and social media at arm's length, not least because of her own negative experiences with them.

Blake's charming smile was replaced in an instant by a frown, but Emily didn't care that her response vexed him.

'I hope to see you tomorrow – 9 a.m. sharp, please,' she said, standing up abruptly, wanting to get back to her proper work.

Blake also stood up and gave her a curt nod.

'Nine a.m. tomorrow it is then, Emma,' he said, his voice sullen and gravelly with irritation at her refusal to pander to him.

'Emily,' she said through gritted teeth.

'Emily,' he repeated with a smirk, then sauntered out of the front door and hopped in the black SUV waiting for him, still illegally parked in front of the centre on the red lines. Emily closed the door and sighed. Not even the jolly twinkling of the Christmas lights could lift her spirits after that experience.

She was dreading the next two weeks.

I'm dreading the next two weeks, Blake thought, as he was driven away in the SUV. He couldn't believe he was going to have to spend time in the dank, shabby centre, surrounded by tacky Christmas decorations, whilst being accosted by weirdos and community oddballs. He felt an intense rush of relief to leave and slide into the car, cracking open a bottle of Evian and trying to wash away even the thought of the instant coffee, which had left a bad taste in his mouth despite the fact he hadn't actually drunk any.

He shuddered to think of the type of people he would be working with. At first, he'd felt a glimmer of optimism to meet Emily; she'd looked like the right age for his main target audience. He'd even been hoping that she might be a fan, but she had appeared obviously disinterested, unimpressed and underwhelmed by his presence. Even turning on the charm for his photo request hadn't worked on her, and he was still smarting at her blunt refusal. Although he could grudgingly admit that she was attractive, with her tousled chocolate-brown hair and honey-coloured eyes, she was also oddly dressed, rude, uptight and was clearly going to be a massive stick-in-the-mud.

He leaned back against the cool leather seat and sighed

as his phone rang, shrill and persistent, breaking the peaceful silence of the car.

'Hello, Mother,' he said as he answered, trying to infuse his voice with a little false enthusiasm for the sake of politeness. 'What a nice surprise to hear from you.'

'Blake!' Mariella's voice trilled down the phone, along with the sound of ice cubes clinking against a glass. 'We're in London!'

Blake closed his eyes at the unwelcome news that his parents were in the UK. Normally they spent most of their time in Beverley Hills, and even though his mother was British, she preferred the LA climate and company, always bemoaning the dark, cold days of the British winter.

'How lovely,' he said flatly. 'What brings you over here?'

'We have a premier to attend, amongst a few other events,' Mariella explained. 'We're staying at the Dorchester, our usual suite. Come by this evening, dear, won't you?'

Blake rubbed his hand across his eyes. 'I'll stop by later tonight,' he said.

He hadn't seen his parents for months, and he knew they would have something to say about the hotel incident and the negative press. He also knew he could look forward to their usual grilling over his somewhat turbulent love life. For all his parents' faults and their terrible parenting skills, he had to hand it to them when it came to romance. They were one of the longest-coupled pairs in Hollywood, still madly in love and fiercely committed to one another. In the showbiz world, they were a rarity. It was just a shame, Blake thought, that their love for each other was so all-encompassing that it had never left them with much to share with him.

'Dan, I'll need you to drive me to the Dorchester tonight,' Blake said to the driver, who nodded without a word, knowing that Blake didn't like small talk. It was times like these Blake regretted not having a personal assistant to quickly organise a prior engagement that would mean he could miss having to see his parents. Unfortunately, his last assistant left a few weeks ago, storming out wailing about his "moods" and "sniping", and he hadn't replaced her yet. Blake tutted at the memory of her hysterical overreaction and made a mental note to find someone else soon.

He rested his head back as the car wound its way through traffic-choked London streets towards the leafy suburbs of Richmond upon Thames, where he was renting a house. He gazed out of the window, watching Christmas lights slide by, blurred by condensation. Blake laced his hands together, swallowed hard, and tried not to think about how much he wanted a drink before he went to see his parents.

Chapter Three

Emily curled up on the sofa, resting her head against River's chest, soothed by the gentle sound of his heart beating and the rise and fall of his breathing, as calming as a waltz. She let out a sigh of contentment at having him close, not paying much attention to the wildlife documentary he'd picked for them to watch that evening. As much as she liked animals, she wasn't really interested in learning about life in an ant colony, although River seemed rapt as she stared up at him.

'Are you going to keep the beard?' she murmured.

'Hmmm?' He looked down at her with a distracted smile.

'The beard? Are you going to keep it?' she asked, extending a hand and running a finger gently down the side of his face, where he was proudly sporting a straggly beard; a memento of his most recent trek into the Bolivian rainforest.

'I might do,' he said, stroking it absently. 'It saves on razors and shaving cream, way more eco-friendly.'

She nodded, a little disappointed. If she were honest, she preferred him without the facial hair, although she still found him attractive with it. He was a wiry six-foot-four-inches, with an unruly mop of mahogany hair and eyes the colour of the ocean, which danced when he was passionate about something. And he was passionate about so many things, including her – she hoped.

She allowed the soporific narration about the ants wash over her, not really paying attention to it. She stayed comfortably nestled against River when the documentary ended and he pondered what to watch next. He flicked through the channels, muttering to himself, and there, bright and bold and marvellous on the screen was *Strictly Dancing with Celebs*. Emily whipped her head towards it, the joyful music of the theme tune hitting her with an emotional punch to the stomach. She drew in a ragged breath, staring at the show she generally tried to avoid for the painful memories it inevitably induced.

But Emily found herself drawn to the screen, feeling like a sugar addict in a cake shop, sniffing the icing, desperate for a taste. As River scrolled through his phone to find recommendations on what to watch, Emily was rapt as the first couple started their routine. Her very cells throbbed in time to the beat as the couple began a salsa; it was one of her favourite dances, one of the only dances she had done on her very short *Strictly* stint, all those years ago.

And then it was gone as River changed the channel, completely oblivious to the tears that had gathered in the corners of her eyes. He happily selected another documentary, talking animatedly about the flora and fauna of Latin America, while Emily sat mute and melancholy, held static by the clash of emotions she felt. It took an hour of watching River's rainforest documentary to help her feel calmer, although her sadness remained at the tantalising glimpse of the career she had chosen to walk away from.

River sat up excitedly, knocking her from her comfortable position against him. 'Look! It's the national park in Costa Rica I was talking about the other day!' he exclaimed, jabbing a finger at the screen. 'It's next on my list.'

She looked at the landscape unfolding on the screen. 'It's beautiful,' she murmured, taking in the swathes of mountainous, dense jungle and sweeping golden sands. 'But you've only just got back from two months in Bolivia. I guess you're not going anywhere *too* soon?' she asked, slightly alarmed.

He chuckled and put a finger under her chin to tilt her head up towards him, gazing into her eyes. 'I'm a free spirit, my angel,' he said, with a boyish grin. 'When I get those itchy feet, I just have to get going.'

She nodded, pushing back a strand of hair from her forehead. 'I just hope your feet aren't too itchy right now,' she said, smiling weakly at his spirit of adventure and hoping he wouldn't go anywhere before Christmas.

'You should come with me next time I go away,' he said. 'It would be amazing for you. You would see so much ...' he trailed off.

She shook her head. 'It's a lovely thought but the community centre has a lot going on, and it's difficult to take more than a week off at a time,' she explained, thinking of all the clients, all the volunteers, all the work to do. Taking time off was nearly impossible and had been for the past few years, not that she begrudged giving her best to her job and to the people she helped. Her stomach knotted with stress at just the idea of trying to organise a proper stretch of time off to go away with River, especially as she was behind in so many things already, despite her efforts to keep up with the workload.

River glanced round at the photos of her siblings that

proudly adorned the walls of her childhood home. 'Your family are such adventurers, Emily,' he said, looking at her with affection. 'It's time you got out and saw the world too, you know? It would enhance your views, change you as a person.'

'I don't want to change,' she mumbled, slightly hurt by his condescending tone and the comparison with her siblings, and wishing he hadn't said it. She knew her family were high-achievers, globe-trotters and philanthropists, while she had turned her back on her dream dancing career for something much less high-profile. She had her reasons for doing so, not that she had ever explained them to River. As much as she liked him, she was sure he wouldn't understand why she was so committed to the centre, even though her job stressed her out and paid her peanuts.

'My job is important and I'm needed here,' she insisted, trying to push away the encroaching feeling of inadequacy that crept over her every time someone drew comparisons between her and her siblings.

He shook his head in bemusement. 'Well, promise me you'll think about it.' He leaned in to give her a kiss.

'Only if you promise to think about staying around for a while,' she murmured, before his lips met hers.

⋆ BLAKE ⋆

Blake strolled through the doors of the Dorchester. He looked straight ahead, unimpressed by the luxurious surroundings, and ignored people's stares. No matter where he went, people always stared. He had gotten used to it and had learned to zone it out over the years.

He passed through the ornate lobby, murmuring with the hushed voices of people checking in and out, and where the gold detailing on the marble pillars glimmered in the gentle lighting. In every corner there were oversized vases of flowers, their petals perfuming the air, the selection carefully chosen to reflect the Christmas season, with blooms of scarlet roses nestling alongside crisp white poinsettias, studded with red berries and sprays of forest-green foliage. Blake ignored these pleasant seasonal reminders and headed directly for his parents' suite, marching quickly, his footsteps resounding business-like and brisk on the marble tiles. Although it was a social visit, he didn't expect it to be a pleasant one, and he wanted to get it over with.

'Mr Harris, sir!' An eager voice interrupted his bleak thoughts, and he turned his head to see a member of the concierge team scurrying alongside him, his eyes bright with anticipation and admiration. 'How lovely to see you here this evening,' the man said, having to take two steps for every one Blake took. 'May I assume you're here to see your parents in the Harlequin Penthouse? They did inform us that you might stop by.'

Blake gave him a curt nod. 'Yes,' he said brusquely.

'Very well, sir. Is there anything you need?'

Blake shook his head. 'No,' he said and carried on walking, leaving the employee behind him with a distinct air of disappointment at the unfulfilling encounter. Blake already knew where to go, having stayed there before himself. It wasn't his favourite hotel in London, but he appreciated the spectacular view of Hyde Park that the Penthouse afforded. His parents were currently savouring the view themselves as they stood outside on the private terrace, his mother's carefree laughter drifting through the evening to him as the Penthouse butler let him in.

Blake walked out to them, the frosty evening air greeting him, making his skin tingle with cold. Hyde Park loomed before him, the vast expanse of dark verdant green a contrast to the glass and concrete city that enveloped it. The sun had crept away meekly that evening, the sunset splendour robbed by foggy cloud, and the city felt dank and damp.

'Mother,' he said, greeting Mariella with a kiss on the cheek. She was draped in fur, a glass of champagne in her hand and a string of pearls luminous at her neck.

Blake never failed to be impressed by how young his mother looked. A stringent salmon-based diet, face creams made of diamonds, and subtle surgical tweaks and procedures kept her looking barely fifty, even though she was nearing seventy – something she would never admit to.

'Blake, how lovely to see you.' She pressed her cheek against his and Blake could smell her signature fragrance; a unique blend of oils made especially in her honour in Saudi Arabia – the gift of a Prince who was enamoured with her.

His father turned to him with a grin, a set of perfect white teeth bright against his tanned skin; the healthy glow courtesy of the LA sunshine. Cole Harris was rakishly handsome, although he was now entirely silver-haired, and Blake knew he owed his own charm and good looks to his American father. 'Hey son.' He slapped Blake on the shoulder. 'What a view, eh? I just love London, especially at this time of year,' he said in his Californian drawl – something which Blake hadn't inherited thanks to his English nannies and schooling in the UK.

Blake nodded. 'Wonderful,' he muttered dryly, not really caring about the view and certainly not about the time of year.

'What are you drinking?' Cole asked, reaching for the champagne bottle he had beside him, nestled in an ice bucket – not that the ice was really necessary given the frozen air which surrounded them.

'No alcohol, thanks,' said Blake, with a shake of his head. 'Rehab, remember?'

Cole put a hand to his mouth. 'Of course.' He signalled to the butler who stood discreetly in the shadows of the terrace.

'I'll have a Coke,' Blake said, and the butler retreated silently and swiftly. The desire for a real drink burned quietly in his brain, but he pushed it firmly away and tore his eyes from the champagne bottle. Rehab had been rough and he had no desire to repeat the experience by falling off the wagon now. He took a deep breath, clenched his fists several times, and tried to focus on the view before them.

'So, you're not planning on trashing *this* room, are you?' Cole said with a wink and a slight smirk, and Blake prickled with irritation at his father's inability to take anything seriously.

Mariella tutted, also unimpressed at Cole's joviality. 'It's not funny, darling,' she said. She placed a hand on Blake's arm, her ice-blue eyes narrowed with concern. 'Really, the headlines were awful. What on earth were you thinking?'

'It was … a combination of things,' Blake muttered, his forehead creasing with a frown. He didn't particularly want to dwell on the memory of that night, where his smouldering rage and frustration had been ignited by vodka in a fiery fury that had overtaken his senses.

Mariella stared at him, and he could sense her disappointment from the slight downturn at the corners of her mouth. 'Do you *have* to do the community sentence?' she asked.

Blake coughed, and was thankful for the glass of Coke handed to him by the butler. He took a gulp, welcoming the tacky sweetness against his teeth and the bright burst of the bubbles in his throat.

'I start tomorrow,' he responded, shuddering as he thought about the drab centre from earlier that day.

'Well, maybe it'll be a good experience.' Cole smiled faintly.

'I doubt it,' Blake said. 'But it has to be done. Judge's orders.'

'Just be careful,' Mariella warned, waving a manicured finger at him. 'There will be all sorts of people there, some could be dangerous, or even contagious.' She wrinkled her nose at the thought of it. 'Make sure you use plenty of hand sanitiser,' she added helpfully.

'What are your plans while you're in London?' Blake asked, remembering what his mother had said on the phone but desperate to change the subject.

'A premier, a few interviews, a charity benefit,' Mariella said breezily. 'The usual things really. Then we're going back to LA.'

'Although maybe we could take the plane to Tuscany instead? After all, a special occasion is coming up ...' Cole said, nuzzling her neck, and Blake tried not to make a face, wishing they didn't have to always be *so* overtly affectionate with each other.

'Oh yes, our anniversary!' Mariella trilled. She turned to Blake with a smile. 'Forty years. Can you believe it?'

Cole grinned broadly. 'It still feels like yesterday that we met.' He stared at Mariella lovingly and stroked her hair while she sighed and touched a hand gently to his chin. Standing before the city skyline, silhouetted against the starry sky, it was almost like a scene from one of their famous romantic movies, but Blake was unmoved and resisted the urge to roll his eyes.

While he was glad they were still happily married, their overwhelming affection for each other had never left much room for him. He always felt like the intruder, an unwanted third wheel; a suspicion that was confirmed to him when they shipped him off to boarding schools and nannies from a young age. He knew that his parent's great love affair had never included plans for a child. He supposed he should be grateful that they kept him at all, not that they had a choice, as his mother found out about the pregnancy when it was too late to do anything about it. She had told him so when he was sixteen and she'd been warning him about the perils of not using contraception. He wasn't surprised by her confession and tucked away the hurt he felt in a small, sore spot in his heart, hidden by teenage bravado and sullen machismo. Since then, his parents had been open with him about the fact that he had been an accident, his father sometimes even joking about it, never realising that each time they mentioned it that he felt wounded all over again.

He thought that his parents had a small measure of affection for him now, and they seemed to like him more as an adult that they could hold a conversation with, but they would never be able to fully heal that sore spot caused by their casual emotional negligence from his early years. He wasn't sure he could wholeheartedly forgive them, though he had spent thousands of dollars and pounds on therapy to help him to do so – but they *were* his parents and he had no other family, so he tried to make the best of their relationship.

Mariella took a sip of champagne and gave Blake a sympathetic look. 'I do hope you find someone to settle with,' she said. 'I'd really prefer not to attend any more of your weddings until you are absolutely sure you've found The One.'

Cole nodded. 'They were fantastic parties, don't get us wrong. Especially the Indian wedding with Anita, what a riot! But it would be nice to go to the next one knowing the marriage might last the distance.'

'Okay, well, I'll let you know,' Blake said sarcastically, prickling at his parents' criticisms, but knowing that they had a point. Three failed marriages at the age of thirty-two wasn't his best achievement. He drained his Coke with a swift gulp. 'I have to go. I've got a big day tomorrow.'

'You only just got here!' Mariella exclaimed.

'I'm very much in demand, lots of things to do. I'll see you before you go back to LA.' Blake turned and walked away from his parents, leaving them to their champagne and their ever-lasting romance.

Chapter Four

+ EMILY +

Emily checked her watch with an irritated sigh. It was almost 9.45 a.m. and her newest "volunteer" hadn't turned up yet. The drop-in session was almost at capacity, with most of the chairs and tables full, and people were still trooping in through the door, eager to escape the cold.

Emily had a policy of never turning people away unless she absolutely had to. She knew how much people needed the centre, and despite the cloudless blue skies, the lacklustre sun couldn't chase away the freezing bite in the air. Emily couldn't bear the thought of her service users, especially the ones who lived on the streets, braving the wind and the rock-hard pavement, and even those who had accommodation might not be able to afford heating or decent food. She carried on allowing people to enter. The noise level increased, and as was so often the case on crowded days, so did people's tensions. The din drowned out the Christmas music playing in the background, so she could only hear snatches of Shakin' Stevens and Wham! amongst the babble of voices and clanging of plates and cups.

Emily flitted from person to person, trying to chat in between her duties, hoping that some warm words would help people to feel welcome.

'No! I have not finished!' she heard Pavel's insistent voice ring out and turned to see him clutching a newspaper, his eyes wide with indignation as Johnny clasped one corner of it.

'Look mate, you put it down and left it. I want to read the sports pages!' Johnny's bellow in reply to Pavel's panicky territorialism made Emily wince. She hurried over and put a hand on Johnny's arm.

At six-foot-three he towered over her, but she wasn't afraid of him. Johnny was like an overgrown child. He was quick to lose his temper, and things could easily escalate when he was angry, but she knew how to handle him.

'Guys,' she said in her best soothing tone, keeping her voice level and low. 'There are plenty of newspapers to go around. There's no need to kick up a fuss about this one.'

'But he left it!' Johnny said insistently. He ran a large hand agitatedly through his thick brown hair, leaving tufts of it sticking up erratically.

'For one second!' Pavel cried. 'Not even a whole minute, and then you grab and take like you own!' His English became more fractured when he was angry or upset, and he often peppered his sentences with his native Bulgarian when that happened. Emily could see from his clenched fists and tense jaw that he was getting aggravated, and she knew she needed to nip this argument in the bud quickly before things got any worse.

Emily turned to Johnny. 'Let me get you another newspaper,' she said calmly.

To her satisfaction, both men fell silent, and she thought she had resolved the matter, till she realised that they were no longer looking at her or each other. Their eyes were drawn behind her, to the figure standing in the entrance to the hall: the new "volunteer", the world-famous Blake Harris, who had finally shown up for his shift.

He walked over, clad in skinny black jeans and a T-shirt, hands in his pockets, with a smattering of stubble and a wolfish grin on his face. 'Sorry I'm late, Em,' he said nonchalantly. 'Hey, guys,' he said, extending an arm and shaking both Johnny and Pavel's hands as they gawped at him. 'I'm Blake. Nice to meet you.'

Emily clenched her jaw in annoyance at Blake's timekeeping and his insincere apology to her.

Johnny let out a huge guffaw, making Emily jump slightly. 'Bloody hell!' he yelled. 'It's you … that actor.' He shook his head, his eyes wide in disbelief. The noise in the hall had faded as people watched with interest, some craning their necks to take a look.

Blake nodded. 'That's right. I'll be here for a few days, helping out.'

'That's nice, very kind, you are good man,' said Pavel, nodding with approval, the argument over the newspaper forgotten.

Blake smiled. 'Well, I've always said it's important to give something back,' he said, with faux-humility that made Emily grind her teeth.

There was a gradual rise in the conversation in the hall again as people turned back to their drinks and their food, and Emily beckoned to Blake and took him to one side.

'Sorry I'm late,' he said, though Emily thought he didn't sound apologetic at all. 'I got held up. Paparazzi haranguing me.' He rolled his eyes. 'Speaking of which …' He brandished his phone and held it out in front of himself to take a selfie, angling the phone to try to get the best side of him.

Emily reached out and lowered his hand with hers. 'I thought we spoke about this?' she said. 'I'm not sure people will be comfortable—'

She was interrupted by Johnny bounding up to them. 'Can I get a selfie?' he asked eagerly, and Blake looked at her with a raised eyebrow.

'Of course,' he said to Johnny, and took the photo as Emily watched with mute annoyance.

He turned back to her. 'You were saying …?' He trailed off. A small, smug smile was playing around the edges of his lips.

She gave him a cool stare in return. 'Mr Harris, given that you were running late, I'd really like you to get started. Let me get you an apron, and I'm pretty sure I can find *lots of work* for you to do today.'

She thought with satisfaction at the plates that would pile up for washing and the toilets needing to be cleaned. Blake could take his selfies, but boy was she going to make him work for the positive publicity. She was no sucker for his movie-star looks and Hollywood charm. If he thought he was in charge here and could get one over on her, she would show him that he was very much mistaken.

＊ BLAKE ＊

Blake looked with dismay at the apron Emily offered him. He fingered the worn, faded material, and wrinkled his nose at the unidentifiable stains that marred the fabric.

'Thanks,' he said, as courteously as he could manage through gritted teeth. He pulled it over his T-shirt and tied it around his waist, feeling that he would have to go home and burn his clothes, even though they were designer.

'Why don't we get you started in the kitchen?' Emily said, with what appeared to be a delighted gleam in her eyes, and he followed her unwillingly, glaring daggers into her back.

'Hi, Fernando,' she said as she walked into the kitchen.

A man was standing before the oven, bobbing up and down with eagerness, his hands flitting over the steaming saucepans on the hob. He was short in stature, but his enthusiasm seemed to fill the room as he said 'Nearly ready!' and turned around to Emily.

'This is Blake, he's volunteering with us for a few weeks,' she said, gesturing towards him.

Fernando gave him a polite nod. 'Nice to meet you, Blake. *Mucho gusto,*' he said.

'*El placer es mio,*' Blake said smoothly. He had learned Spanish from a young age, and the words flowed without a second thought.

Fernando looked enthralled and he clapped his hands together. 'You speak Spanish!' he exclaimed with joy.

'*Claro que si,*' Blake said, giving Emily a sideways glance.

She looked unimpressed. 'Fabulous. Blake, it would be great if you could help Fernando serve up the food and clean up the pots and plates too.' She turned and left the kitchen without another word.

Blake watched her walk away. She wore knee-high brown boots tucked over jeans, and her hair was gathered messily at the nape of her neck, a few dark curls falling down in contrast to the paleness of her cream jumper. Her boots, thick-soled and designed for cold weather rather than sexiness, thudded quickly away as she hurried to her next task. Blake turned to Fernando.

'What can I help you with?' he asked, glancing around at the kitchen. What he really wanted to do was have a decent coffee, but he refrained from asking, knowing it was pointless when they only had instant.

Fernando gestured to the serving hatch. 'I'll dish up, you pass them out,' he said, and he began portioning out large bowlfuls of steaming porridge, and plates with beans, sausages and fried potatoes. Blake eyed the food suspiciously. It was sturdy, hearty fare, made with cheap, bulk-bought ingredients – a far cry from the cuisine he usually sampled at the best London restaurants. He stood at the serving hatch, where a queue had formed, and passed out the bowls.

'Here you are, here's yours, enjoy, *bon appétit*,' he said, already bored, but feeling that he was very gracious as he handed over the food. He was a little surprised that the people accepting it didn't show more gratitude. He got a smile here and there, and the odd nod of thanks, but he had expected people to be gushing with thankfulness. Instead, they practically snatched their bowls and tucked in hungrily, practically inhaling the food with an urgency he had never seen before. Blake was used to dining with people who could make a lettuce leaf last an entire meal, at restaurants where portions were thumb-sized and astronomically priced. Here, there was a faint air of desperation that he guessed only genuine hunger could provoke.

After they had served all the people in the hall, Fernando nudged his elbow. 'Have some – it's my special banana and cinnamon porridge.' He handed him a bowl with a nod and a warm smile that crinkled his eyes. 'The volunteers get to eat too. Emily insists we have the food as well.'

'Where do I eat?' Blake asked, taking the bowl and staring at the contents. It wasn't beautifully presented, just a splodge of white goop, but he had to admit that it smelled good. 'Is there a staff room or something?'

Fernando laughed. 'No, you can eat in the hall.'

Blake looked around doubtfully, seeing only a few scattered free chairs squished in between people he would prefer not to be too close to.

Fernando ushered him out of the kitchen. 'Go, eat!' he commanded, and Blake clutched his bowl and perched awkwardly on the nearest seat to the door. He smiled at the pinched woman next to him, and ate a few spoonfuls of the porridge, pleasantly surprised to find it was edible.

'You're in films, aren't you?' A woman opposite him leaned forward with an intense stare on her weary face.

Blake nodded. 'That's right. Are you a fan?' He turned on his best smile.

He was taken aback when the woman let out a harsh bark of a laugh. 'I don't watch much in the way of films,' she said, grinning at him with cigarette-stained teeth. 'But I know you, you're always in the papers. What are you doing here?'

'Just a little volunteering. Giving something back to the community,' he said.

'Nothing to do with that hotel incident then?' she asked, giving him a wry look.

Blake coughed uncomfortably. 'That was really a misunderstanding,' he said warily. 'I'm just glad to have the opportunity to be here today and meet you all.'

The woman's face softened, her suspicious look replaced by a small smile. 'I'm Linda,' she said.

'Lovely to meet you, Linda,' Blake said. He could feel people staring at him, sizing him up, wondering what he was doing there. Blake felt totally out of his comfort zone, so he did what his father always told him to do – *take control and get the attention you want for the right reasons*. It had been advice that had always worked for him. Leaning back in his chair, he shouted out towards the kitchen, 'Fernando, *amigo*, this food is fabulous! Five stars!'

Johnny shouted out 'Hear, hear!' and there was a spontaneous scattering of applause. Fernando appeared in the serving hatch and beamed with delight at Blake's praise, giving him a thumbs up.

Blake smiled at the response. He was good at winning people over when he put his mind to it, if he wanted to. As Blake glanced up, he saw Emily leaning against the entrance to the hall, giving him a frosty look, her lips pressed together. She held his gaze for a moment then turned and walked away, clutching her clipboard and her mug of instant coffee, her footsteps in time with the terrible Christmas music jangling on the radio. Blake could tell by her manner that she was unimpressed with his efforts.

Oh well, he thought to himself, taking a few more mouthfuls of porridge. *Can't win them all.*

✦ EMILY ✦

Emily kept a close watch on Blake until the drop-in session ended. She could see straight through his act.

She knew he didn't really care at all about the service users and their needs, but they couldn't seem to pick up on that as he chatted and laughed and strolled around the hall, greeting them like they were his fans while they lapped it up. To her increasing frustration, he also ignored her advice about taking photographs too. In truth, it wasn't just the privacy of the service users she wanted to protect. She knew that if he put the photos on his social media, they would only show the positives – a cosy hall and a cup of tea served by a famous face – and not the simmering despair, hunger, anger and tension that bubbled just below the surface of so many of these people's lives. It would be a feel-good, look-good post, not a truthful representation of the day-to-day in a local charity that was desperately trying to make a difference in some very broken lives. If she was honest, she also didn't want to be photographed herself – although that was for her own selfish reasons.

Emily leaned against the door frame of the entrance to the hall, looking around at the chalk-white walls covered in scuff marks, the harsh lighting they had tried to soften with Christmas fairy lights, the marked and stained wooden floor, which hundreds of feet had trodden on as people came in looking for a little respite from their struggles. She remembered when she started at the community centre, not knowing how the difficulties of others would shape her life, and how those few weeks at the centre had impacted her so entirely that she ended up staying and working her way up to manager. It was a world away from dancing, from the bright lights and sequins of *Strictly* that she had experienced so briefly. But she had been ready for a change, willing to give back, needing to make amends, and Blake didn't seem to be of the same mindset as she had been all those years ago.

She sighed heavily and her colleague, Lizzie, looked round in surprise as she walked by.

'What's the matter?' she asked.

'Oh, nothing,' Emily murmured. 'Just trying to keep an eye on Mr Hollywood over there.' She rolled her eyes in Blake's direction.

Lizzie stared across at him and pushed her glasses up on her nose. 'He's doing well. Everyone seems to like him,' she remarked.

Emily shook her head. 'I don't think he really cares at all.' She turned towards Lizzie so that the other volunteers wouldn't overhear.

Lizzie shrugged. 'Either way, whether he cares or not, he has to complete his community order and we're stuck with him. Come on, Emily – it's not that bad.' She ran a hand over her greying blonde hair, which she complained that no product could tame, and gave Emily a warm smile. 'The drop-in can be a tough environment for a new volunteer and he seems to be doing okay. Plus, he's very easy on the eye.'

Emily gave her a faint smile. 'I suppose so,' she said, not wanting to admit that of course she found Blake attractive. She was only human, and he was undeniably gorgeous. Even dressed in jeans and a T-shirt, he stood out amongst the crowd.

Lizzie widened her eyes. 'You suppose? Just look at those cheekbones, those eyes …' she sighed dreamily. 'If I were twenty years younger. And not married …' She giggled.

Emily cleared her throat. 'Objectively yes, of course he's

very handsome – but speak to him for five minutes Lizzie, and you'll see what I see, trust me.'

'And what's that?'

Emily turned away from Blake and towards her colleague, speaking in hushed tones which still were sharp with annoyance. 'That he shows no remorse for the actions which led him here, and he's a self-obsessed, arrogant, rude prick.'

'Who is?'

A voice behind Emily made her jump, and she turned to see Blake standing there. Her cheeks flushed at what he might have heard as he'd crossed the room to join them.

'Um ...' she stammered. 'We're just discussing—'

'A mutual friend of ours,' Lizzie interjected, and Emily shot her a grateful look.

'Really?' Blake looked unconvinced and Emily knew he wasn't fooled. 'Poor guy,' he said, with a wary look.

Emily shifted her feet awkwardly. 'We should really start to close up,' she said, brushing past Blake and heading towards the door, where another volunteer, Gloria, was standing.

'Such a busy day but what a good time we've all had,' Gloria trilled, and Emily's spirits couldn't help but be lifted by her bright smile. Emily knew that Gloria's life wasn't easy, as a single mum from Zimbabwe who was looking for work and struggling to make ends meet, but Emily admired her tenacity and determination to help those even less fortunate than herself.

'We need to start closing up now,' Emily instructed, and Gloria nodded, helping to usher out people who were still in the hall.

Emily's feet ached and her calves felt tight. She loved

the drop-in sessions, but she was always exhausted when they were over, and there was still the cleaning and tidying to do. A painful knot in her stomach reminded her that she hadn't eaten anything that day – there just hadn't been time. She swallowed hard and scrunched her toes inside her boots, momentarily distracted from her physical tiredness by the sound of Lizzie laughing. She glanced over and saw Blake chatting animatedly with her, as Lizzie looked up at him with what could only be described as an adoring expression.

Emily shook her head, unable to understand how even sensible, smart, fierce Lizzie could be distracted from Blake's clear personal failings by his good looks. Emily's eyes traced the tattoos on his tanned arms as he ran a hand through his midnight-black hair, which fell over his forehead. He turned from Lizzie's attentions and caught Emily looking at him. He raised an eyebrow and flashed her a grin, and she quickly glanced away, irritated that he'd noticed her looking and might think she was gawping at him the way everyone else seemed to.

Emily turned to help Darren with clearing the hall and saying goodbye to people. By the time the last service user had filed out of the front door it was nearing 3 p.m., but there was still much more work to be done. She opened up the cleaning cupboard and handed out the sprays, the brooms and the mops to her trusty team. Fernando, Darren, Gloria and Lizzie all scurried to work, and Emily herself rolled up her sleeves and grabbed a broom.

She waved at Blake, who was loitering near the front door, holding out an antibacterial spray and a cloth to him. 'Here you go,' she said as he grasped the cleaning items, the charming grin he wore when talking to Lizzie replaced by a blank expression as he looked at the spray bottle. 'We wipe everything down after drop-in. Start with the tables in the hall,' she instructed.

Blake coughed. 'See, here's the thing, I have a meeting to get to,' he said. 'I really can't stay later than three. Terribly sorry.' A smirk lingered on his lips as he handed the spray and cloth back to her.

'Oh,' Emily said. 'It would have been helpful to know that beforehand.' She didn't believe him for a second, but she was in no mood to interrogate him when there was still plenty of work to do. 'In that case, can you follow me to the office for a quick debrief before you go?'

She beckoned for Blake to follow her and he did so reluctantly, checking his watch with an air of impatience.

Emily closed the door behind them. 'So, Mr Harris, how did you find the first day?' she questioned, sitting at the desk and folding her hands together.

'It was great,' he said flatly. His charm and enthusiasm were gone now they were alone, and he looked at her with a cool, calm gaze, his eyes stone-grey and his expression unreadable.

'I thought you did well,' Emily said. 'But I do want to point some things out to you to bear in mind.'

Blake arched an eyebrow and didn't say anything.

'Firstly, if you are running late, please phone and let me know. I rely on everyone being here on time to help set up and so I can brief you all on anything you need to prepare for.'

Blake nodded. 'Okay, fair enough.'

'Secondly, I'm glad that you found Fernando's cooking so delicious, but we do try to refrain from shouting in the hall.'

Blake laughed incredulously. 'Really? You're telling me off for complimenting the food?'

Emily pressed her lips together at his mocking tone. 'There are times when tensions run high between service users,' she snapped in reply. 'We don't want volunteers shouting around the place as well. We try to keep things calm. There are people who come here who have experienced violence and war and all sorts of trauma, and raised voices can be upsetting.'

Blake twisted his beautiful features into a scowl. 'I was just saying something positive.'

'Yes, but you were sitting next to Bella, and your sudden shout startled her. Didn't you see that?'

'I don't remember talking to anyone called Bella,' Blake said, looking confused.

'She was the thin woman with dark hair next to you. She moved away after that as I think you made her uncomfortable,' Emily insisted.

Blake shifted impatiently in his seat and huffed. 'Right, fine, so no raised voices. Got it. Anything else?'

Emily resisted the urge to frown at him, knowing it would look unprofessional. She had dealt with uncooperative people before, and she had to treat Blake the same way she would treat anyone else – firmly, professionally and courteously. She fixed her face into a neutral expression. 'That's all. Thank you for your help today,' she said, her voice tight with the effort of remaining calm.

Blake got up and walked out of the office, waving to the other volunteers as if he had known them for months rather than just hours. 'Bye, guys!' he shouted loudly, with a backwards glance at Emily. She clenched her fists under the desk as Blake walked out, watched in awe by the volunteers, and clambered into his SUV, again illegally parked and covered with tickets.

Emily left the office to retrieve her broom and passed Darren, who was watching Blake leave.

'What a guy,' Darren said dreamily.

She shook her head. 'What an arsehole,' she muttered under her breath as Blake sped away.

Chapter Five

Blake sipped his black coffee and took a moment to gather his thoughts while the car pulled up outside the community centre for his second day. He hadn't enjoyed the 7 a.m. alarm that morning, and he'd resented every second he had spent sitting in the London traffic rather than lounging in bed at his luxurious rented home. He breathed in the aroma of the coffee, willing the caffeine to start coursing through his body and wake him up.

He was still smarting at Emily's attitude from yesterday. He had done the work she had asked, served the food, chatted to the strange people in the project, even worn the apron – he'd expected a little gratitude. Instead, her cold criticism of his efforts had rankled him all last night and he still felt pissed off and irritable.

He sighed and took another gulp of coffee, knowing it would be the last decent one he had that day.

'Have a good day, Mr Harris,' Dan said politely, as he opened the door and jumped out, acknowledging the driver's pleasantries with a short nod before the frosty air enveloped him. A cold fog hung low over the streets, making everything seem grey, sapped of colour and warmth.

'Mr Harris!' A photographer leaning against the wall of the community centre leapt to action, scurrying towards him, brandishing his camera like a weapon. Blake nodded at him and paused so he could get a few shots, as had been agreed with both the photographer

47

and his agent. Blake switched on a bright, false smile, and tried to look like he was walking towards the front door with both purpose and pleasure. Alice had assurances that the papers wouldn't print the location of his community service, but a few good photos of him looking cheerful and enthusiastic on the way in would go a long way.

He rang the bell and the door swung open, Emily standing behind it.

'Morning,' he said, trying to be polite. He fixed a neutral expression on his face, although he really wanted to give her a cold glare for her rude ingratitude yesterday.

'Morning,' she replied. As she spotted the photographer, she frowned and quickly turned away, closing the door behind him. 'I hope the papers wont print where you're working.' A look of concern flitted across her face. 'I don't want hoards of your fans accosting us here.'

Blake shook his head. 'I'm sure they won't,' he said. 'They just want a good photo, the details don't really matter.'

'Right.' She looked unconvinced.

Blake gave her outfit a fleeting glance, surprised at how shabby she looked that day. Even for a community centre manager, he thought she could dress a little more professionally than her current unflattering ensemble of tatty jeans, decorated with a variety of rips and paint splodges, and a baggy black T-shirt with a faded slogan that he couldn't quite make out. Blake squinted at it and she crossed her arms across her chest with an indignant look.

'Oh, I was just trying to see the logo.' He indicated towards her T-shirt, hoping she didn't think he was leering at her, not that he would find someone dressed in such a way remotely attractive, regardless of how pretty she actually was.

'Ah, right,' she said, her expression softening slightly. She stretched out the fabric so he could see the faded lettering.

'Live a life that matters,' he read aloud. 'Who said that?'

'I don't actually know,' Emily admitted, looking down at it. 'But I like the sentiment.' She glanced at him and he nodded as if to agree, but he didn't really care. What mattered to him right now was surviving another day of his community service without catching any communicable diseases, without Emily telling him off and without any weirdos getting too friendly with him.

'We're doing the arts and crafts session this morning,' she said, beckoning him to follow her into the hall. 'You did read the notes about it, right?'

'Um, I can't really remember,' Blake muttered. In fact, he couldn't even recall where the notes were. He had dumped the carefully written binder somewhere in his house and forgotten about it entirely.

'Are those clothes okay to get a bit messy?' she asked him, eyeing his outfit. He looked down at what he was wearing: indigo jeans and a grey cashmere jumper. As casual as his outfit looked, he couldn't hide the small Hugo Boss logo on the jumper.

'Sure.' He shrugged, unbothered by the idea that his outfit probably cost more than her daily wage, and knowing he could always buy more clothes if these ones got ruined.

He walked behind her to the hall where she had already laid out materials for the session.

'We're going to be making some Christmas decorations,' she said, her expression brightening as she indicated the glitter, glue and coloured card that festooned the table.

Blake eyed the materials and suppressed a sigh. He hated crafts, and he hated tacky Christmas decorations. He couldn't think of anything worse to do on a freezing Tuesday.

Emily saw the unenthusiastic look on his face and her smile dimmed a little. 'We make decorations and sell them every year. We don't make much, just a few pounds really, but—' she shrugged '—the people who come to the sessions enjoy themselves and get a feeling of achievement from it.'

'Great.' Blake forced a grin.

He sat down at the table and Emily went to answer the door to the few people who had arrived for the workshop. Blake recognised some of them from the drop-in – Bella, Linda and Johnny – but there were a few new faces too. Emily brought out a few plates of biscuits and turned the Christmas music on. Blake tried not to wince as the tired old classics jangled merrily, the sound from the cheap speakers tinny and thin in the hall.

'All right, Tony?' Johnny bellowed as a bone-thin man slunk in and sat at the end of the table, helping himself to tea from the urn and dumping five spoonfuls of sugar in it. Tony nodded wearily, rubbing a hand over his face. He had a shrunken, hollow look to him, his sallow skin rough with stubble, his eyelids droopy with weariness. Everything about him seemed rough and paper-thin, worn away as if someone had sandpapered him. Blake glanced at him, wondering if he was ill, and hoped it wasn't something he could catch.

Aside from Lizzie occasionally popping in, the session was run by Emily on her own. Blake watched her as she carefully explained the instructions for the decorations. He had to admit that he was impressed by her patience and her optimism given the strange group of people who had turned up, and their clear lack of artistic talent. She encouraged them, smiling and nodding, despite Bella's awkwardness, Tony's refusal to engage and Johnny's horsing around. Blake watched her laughing with Bella, and he wondered how this warm and lively woman was also the same person that kept chastising him so coldly. Emily's thick, wavy hair was pulled up in a messy ponytail, leaving a few strands grazing her cheeks, and her eyes shone as Bella proudly held up a completed bauble.

'Aren't *you* going to make a bauble?' Linda asked him, leaning across the table.

Blake frowned at the polystyrene balls and glitter. 'Crafts aren't really my thing,' he said.

Emily overheard and caught his eye. 'Try,' she mouthed at him, a small frown flitting across her face, and Blake reluctantly reached out to take the materials.

Blake didn't really understand why it mattered that he tried – after all, he wasn't a service user. He suppressed a bored sigh as he slopped some glue and glitter onto the ball, wishing he was anywhere else, preferably somewhere warm with a masseuse on hand. Linda nodded approvingly and even Bella gave him a small smile as he fumbled with the strips of wrapping paper which he clumsily tried to paste around the bauble. The patchwork of coloured paper clumped and wrinkled over the glue he had applied too thickly, and Blake knew it didn't look good. In fact, it looked like a blind monkey could have made it.

'It's not bad,' Linda said kindly, as if reading his mind.

Blake tutted at his bauble and shook his head. 'No one would buy this,' he said, glaring at it, feeling almost offended at how bad it looked and embarrassed that he had made it.

'Maybe you could autograph it?' Johnny suggested with an eager nod. 'That would probably be worth a few quid.'

Blake realised they were all trying to make him feel better, and yet he was the one who was supposed to be helping and encouraging them. After all, they were the losers, the misfits, the poor – not him. He looked at his glitter-marked hands and felt about two-foot tall.

He smiled at Linda and Johnny and nodded. 'I'll try another one,' he said, but as he reached out, he was interrupted by Tony, who suddenly stood up and hurled a ball across the room, where it left a sad trail of silver glitter on the floor.

'What's the point?!' Tony yelled, the sinews on his neck standing out. 'I can't do it, it's rubbish!'

Emily quickly stood up. 'Tony,' she said, calmly. 'You were doing great. It's not rubbish, honestly.'

'Bloody baubles,' he shouted, his eyes wide and strained. 'Load of crap!'

In a second, the atmosphere in the hall had changed. Tony's outburst and wild expression made everyone feel uneasy, even though the Christmas tunes still carried on in the background, Cliff Richard singing on about mistletoe and wine and some other nonsense that Blake didn't care for. He glanced at Linda and Bella, who shrank from the yelling, and even Johnny looked startled.

'Come on mate, sit down,' Johnny said hesitantly to Tony.

Instead, Tony picked up his chair and threw it across the room, where it thudded onto the scuffed floor with a loud metallic twang. Blake looked quickly at Emily, wondering if he should try to help. He had learned martial arts for a movie once, and he was certainly more of a match for this madman than Emily was. She saw him looking and gave a slight motion of her hand as if to say "stay put".

She cleared her throat. 'Come on Tony, let's go,' she said firmly. 'I can't have that in here, you know that.'

Blake was impressed by her calmness. She seemed entirely unruffled and totally in control without even raising her voice. She walked into the hallway and Tony grabbed his backpack and slunk after her. The group in the hall fell silent as they all tried to hear the conversation at the door, but Emily's soft tones weren't perceptible and Tony's ramblings didn't make much sense to any of them.

Johnny leaned over to Blake. 'He's an alcoholic, always on and off the streets,' he said knowingly. 'Probably had too much this morning.'

Blake raised his eyebrows and nodded. He knew what it was like for alcohol to stoke an irrepressible fire inside, to have an urge to throw and damage furniture, people, opportunities, to try to make the outside world hurt as much as the inside of your head did. He felt a wave of unexpected sympathy and understanding for Tony.

Glancing at the others around the table, he could see that they were shaken, their decorations left unfinished, doubt written on their faces.

'Come on then,' he said to the group. 'You have to help

me finish this one.' He held up his efforts with a grin. 'What do you think?'

Bella looked at him with a faint smile and he nudged the botched decoration across to her. 'Can you help me with this?' he asked, turning on a charming smile and trying to ignore the image of Tony's desperate eyes burned into his mind.

✦ EMILY ✦

Emily paused in the hallway, her nerves still jangling from the confrontation with Tony. She took a few deep breaths. She wished she could help Tony, wished she had the right words to say and the time to focus on his needs, but she couldn't allow his behaviour to affect the others. She hated to ask him to leave, but she couldn't handle him and run the craft group as well as supervising Blake.

She sighed and rubbed her forehead with her hand, taking a moment before she went back into the hall, knowing she couldn't leave Blake for too long. She half expected the group to be in disarray, but to her surprise she heard laughter ringing out. Emily was even more taken aback to realise it was Bella's laughter; a rare sound indeed from the meek Romanian.

Emily walked into the hall and saw the group ploughing through the materials, the baubles piling up on the table. Bella was focused on her work with a satisfied smile, and Linda, who was notoriously wary around new people, was having a chatty discussion. Even Johnny was participating in his own loud and clumsy way, humming along to Elton John's 'Step into Christmas'. And at the centre of this merry scene was Blake, passing out materials, regaling the group with anecdotes about Hollywood, seemingly having them all enthralled.

Emily blinked hard, wondering if she was imagining things. It seemed as though her new volunteer wasn't completely hopeless after all.

She re-joined the session and tried to act light-hearted, but her usual enjoyment was dampened by thoughts of Tony, a long-time service user who was constantly on and off the streets and on and off the wagon – someone she and Lizzie had tried to help again and again and again. She wished she could do more, but she knew Tony had to make his own choices. Help couldn't be forced on anyone, Emily knew that better than most. The choice and the determination to change had to come from within. That's how it had been for her, and that's how it would have to be for Tony.

She forced a smile and focused on the baubles, relieved when the session ended and she could collect up the materials, desperate for a cup of tea and a few minutes to think before her next task for the day.

The hall fell silent as the last of the group filed out, and Blake helped her to tidy up, sweeping up the glitter from the floor, and putting the baubles out to dry on newspaper above the radiator. It pumped out a measly stream of heat, barely enough to warm the hall against the bitter chill from outside. Blake touched the lukewarm metal and shook his head. Emily knew the lack of heat was a problem, but the energy costs were so high, budgets were tight and it was the best they could do. She shuddered as she thought of Tony outside in the winter cold, and the guilt she felt about not being able to help him twisted inside her like a knife.

Blake cleared his throat, breaking the silence. 'Are you okay?' he asked.

She looked up at him, pausing as she packed the materials into a box.

'Yeah,' she said. 'I'm just a bit upset by Tony's outburst, although it's not the first time that's happened and probably won't be the last.'

'What's the deal with him?' Blake asked, leaning on his broom. He stared at her with a sombre expression, looking genuinely concerned.

Emily pushed back a strand of hair that had escaped her ponytail. 'He's an ex-serviceman, and has been on and off the streets for a while. He's been through a lot and we're trying to help him, but ...' She trailed off with a despairing shake of her head '... it's tough. We've never been able to persuade him to go to rehab, and every time I think we're making progress it's like he takes a few steps backwards.'

Blake nodded thoughtfully. 'Well, he has to be the one to choose help,' he said, running a hand over the stubble on his chin. 'Rehab has to be his choice or he'll not go through with it. Believe me, I know.' He added the last part in a low voice.

'Speaking from personal experience?' she asked carefully, knowing of course that he was; his entry into rehab had been widely reported by the press.

He glanced at her but didn't quite meet her eyes. 'You could say that,' he said shortly, and she knew the conversation would go no further.

'I was impressed that you got people's minds off what happened,' she said. 'Tony's needs are important, but it's also vital that this is a safe space for others too, and you helped them to feel at ease again. Thank you,' she said warmly, and for the first time the praise she gave him was actually genuinely earned and given.

Blake grinned as he carried on sweeping. 'I did my best,' he said, and he sounded nonchalant, but she got the sense he was at least a little bit pleased with himself as his serious expression brightened, the curve of a smile playing around the corners of his mouth.

She put her hands on her hips and looked around. 'We're pretty much done here. Fernando is coming in to sort out all the food delivery today and plan the menus. Would you be okay to help him out this afternoon? I have a tonne of paperwork to get on with.'

She thought of all the safeguarding reports, monitoring and fundraising information she had to collate, not to mention the budgets that she needed to work on, and her heart sank slightly. She loved working at the centre, but the weight of the admin was wearing her down slightly and it wasn't her strong point, as Rowan frequently pointed out to her. She wished they had the budget for a decent assistant, but it was all on her shoulders and she often felt that she was drowning in the responsibility, completely overwhelmed and constantly in a muddle. Sometimes she woke up in the middle of the night in a panicked sweat remembering that she hadn't filed something correctly.

'No problem,' said Blake. 'I'd be happy to help Fernando this afternoon.'

Emily nodded gratefully and watched him take the box of materials back to the cupboard, wondering if she had misjudged him.

Chapter Six

Blake got out of the car, shivering in the fresh morning air, and checked his watch. He was only a little bit late that morning, so hopefully Emily wouldn't be too pissy about it. Although he wasn't looking forward to another day at the centre, he was pleased with how the crafts session had gone yesterday. The afternoon with Fernando had been slightly dull but he'd managed to sneak off early while Emily was stuck in the office, and he didn't think she'd noticed his absence.

He headed towards the door, avoiding the piles of sludge caught in the gutter. It had snowed last night but not enough for it to settle fully; the only remnants left of the snowfall this morning were the icy slush piles on the side of the road, stained brown and grey by London's grime.

He rapped on the door and Emily opened it for him.

'Morning.' He stepped inside.

She shut the door behind him. 'You left early yesterday,' she said, not even bothering to greet him, her mouth pressed into a thin line and her arms crossed. 'And you're thirty minutes late this morning too.' Gone was the warmth in her eyes that he had seen after the craft session yesterday. She looked tired and annoyed instead, her eyes shadowy and her mouth taut.

'Oh yeah, well, Fernando and I had finished so I thought …' he stopped speaking as she shook her head.

'I'm supervising you here, and you should have come to

58

me. There was plenty more work to be done around the centre. If you want to leave before your day is over, you need to ask,' she said curtly.

Blake couldn't help but scowl at her hectoring tone.

'If I want to go, I'll go,' he snapped back. 'I'm not a child and I don't need your permission to leave. I'm not a prisoner.'

'May I remind you that you would be in prison if it weren't for your community service? Or have you forgotten that a judge ordered you to be here?' she said, her voice sharp and her eyes gleaming with annoyance. An angry flush crept onto her cheekbones, and Blake was briefly preoccupied by the way it warmed her skin – somehow her anger made her look momentarily sexy.

Blake huffed, both distracted and irritated by her, but he couldn't think of a decent response as he knew that she was right. She opened her mouth to speak again but was interrupted by Lizzie, who poked her head out of the office door.

'Hello!' Lizzie chirped, startling them both out of their standoff. 'Emily, is it okay if I borrow Blake for a bit please? I have a task for him.'

Emily widened her eyes in surprise and nodded. 'Of course. Be my guest,' she said, glaring once again at Blake before turning her back to him and walking to the office.

'Follow me!' Lizzie said merrily, oblivious to the tension between them, and Blake followed her down the hall, shooting a dirty look at Emily as she walked away.

'You know how to use a computer, I assume?' Lizzie asked him.

Blake nodded, trying to shake off the encroaching bad mood that Emily had managed to put him in. 'Of course.'

Lizzie pointed at two computers in the corner of the hall, their screens gently flickering. They were boxy and old, and Blake was surprised that two such clunky models could even switch on any more. They were a world away from his razor-thin Apple laptop.

'A couple of people have come in today and I promised I'd help them with some computing, but I have an urgent keyworker matter to deal with,' Lizzie said, peering at him hopefully.

'What's the problem?' Blake asked curiously.

'One of my clients is about to be made homeless.' Lizzie shook her head, suddenly looking fraught. 'I need to get on the phone to the council right away. Perhaps you could help out here until I'm done?'

Blake nodded. 'I can do that,' he said. Although he didn't relish the task at hand, he was grateful he wouldn't have to make more Christmas decorations today.

Lizzie smiled at him and squeezed his arm gratefully, her cheeks turning slightly pink as she did so. 'Gloria is here as well, only her computer skills aren't very good,' she said, lowering her voice and glancing in Gloria's direction.

Gloria looked up from where she was setting up the tea urn. 'I heard that.'

Lizzie bit her lip with a grin. 'Oh well, you know it's true.' She turned to Blake. 'Let me introduce you to who you'll be helping.'

She walked over to a man hovering by the computers. He was looking at them, doubt written across his face. Blake thought he was probably about fifty years old, and he appeared unshaven and out of shape. His cheeks were rough and criss-crossed with spidery red veins, but his sky-blue eyes sparkled out amongst the lines that creased around them. 'Blake, this is Stuart.' Lizzie gestured towards him.

Blake gave him a polite nod. 'Nice to meet you, Stuart.'

Stuart gave him a warm smile and held out a large hand. Blake shook it, and the man's skin felt like sandpaper against his own.

'Stuart is hoping to put together a CV or do some job applications, and he could use a little help,' Lizzie said. 'I'm sure Blake will be able to help you.' She smiled at them both before scurrying off, wrapping her large cardigan around her against the chill of the hall.

Blake turned to the computer. 'Why don't we get started?'

Stuart sat down, looking at Blake carefully. 'You're that actor,' he said, after a moment's pause.

'That's me,' Blake said, hoping he wouldn't have to make too much small talk.

'It's nice of you to help out here.' Stuart hunched his large frame over the computer and shifted on his chair.

Blake smiled graciously. 'Well, it's important to give something back,' he said magnanimously. 'So, what can I help you with?'

Stuart clasped his hands and wound his fingers together. 'I was hoping to put together a CV, maybe apply for some jobs.' He said it uncertainly with an air of apology, and Blake could almost see the lack of self-confidence etched across his face.

'What sort of thing do you do?' Blake asked, loading Microsoft Word and gritting his teeth at how slowly the programme cranked into life.

'I worked in security for a long time but then I got

made redundant,' Stuart explained. 'I haven't been able to find anything for months. No one seems to want to hire a fifty-two-year-old ex-bouncer.' His blue eyes dimmed as a shadow of despair crossed his face. 'I've answered so many job adverts, but it never works out. I barely even get a reply most of the time, let alone an interview. I've applied for everything, I'll do anything. I've got a family to support.'

He looked down at the ground and swallowed hard. Blake felt a wave of pity for him.

'That must be hard,' he said softly.

'You've no idea, mate.' Stuart shook his head. 'It's tough out there. And the bills, the mortgage, they all have to be paid. I'm not proud – I'm a hard worker and I'll take anything I can get as long as it gives me some income.' He shrugged his shoulders and sighed.

Blake had never had money worries and couldn't imagine what it was like, but he felt sorry for this man, who was clearly feeling defeated by his struggles, and who, despite his large frame, seemed small and shrunken, as if he was being compressed by his difficulties.

'Let's see what we can do, shall we?' Blake said, feeling a sudden spark of determination to help, sitting up straight and clicking the mouse with renewed enthusiasm. He tried to stay positive even though the old computer kept freezing and the keyboard was sticky, and even though it took an excruciatingly long time to put together the CV and help Stuart apply for some roles. Blake was often on the verge of losing his patience, and then he remembered that he could go home to his sprawling rented home and healthy bank balance, and Stuart, well, what would he go home to? A family who relied on him, and bills to pay, and no way to pay them. Blake found himself slightly surprised at how much he cared about this crumpled, unemployed, friendly man he had only just met. He wondered whether this was how Emily felt, as he remembered the expression on her face when she was talking to clients at the drop-in; a look that indicated genuine care and concern.

Several hours had passed and Stuart had to leave. Blake stood up, wincing, realising he was stiff and cold and hadn't eaten any lunch, although Gloria had kindly brought him and Stuart multiple cups of tea.

Stuart grabbed his hand and shook it, squeezing it tightly. 'Thank you for all your help,' he said earnestly.

'I hope you find something,' Blake said, and he meant it.

Stuart turned to go and then swivelled round before he left. 'You're a good bloke, Blake.' He smiled, his blue eyes shining once more with renewed hope and optimism.

Blake nodded and watched him amble off, and he couldn't help but smile too. Helping Stuart hadn't been glamorous or exciting, but, now that the tedium was over, he felt a real glow of satisfaction at the morning's work. His time, normally worth thousands of dollars, was paid with nothing more than humble thanks, and it actually felt worth it.

Lizzie bounded up to him with a delighted expression. 'Blake! I just bumped into Stuart as he was leaving. He is so pleased with your help today, thank you so much,' she said.

'It's nothing,' Blake said.

'Have you eaten?' Lizzie asked, and frowned as Blake shook his head.

'Make sure you grab a sandwich from the kitchen,' she

said, waving her own at him, small crumbs flying from her hand and scattering on the floor, which she didn't seem to notice. 'We've had a delivery, and it's important you eat.'

Blake headed to the kitchen and looked at the selection of sandwiches, given away by supermarkets to charity projects on the cusp of their use-by dates. He wrinkled his nose and quickly wolfed down a cheese and ham one before he went in search of Emily to find out his next task for the day. He made his way to the office and poked his head round the door but there was no sign of her.

Gloria saw him peering in the office door and called out to him. 'She's in the other room, preparing for dance class.'

'Dance class?' Blake raised his eyebrows incredulously and tried to suppress a smile at the idea of people like Stuart and Linda dancing.

'It's a passion of hers. Some of the older people in the community like it,' Gloria replied.

Blake could hear the faint sounds of music floating through the air, and he was glad that it wasn't more irritatingly cheerful Christmas music, which set his teeth on edge every year when every radio station insisted on playing it again and again from November onwards. The notes he heard drifting through the silence were unmistakably a waltz, and he followed the sound to one of the smaller side rooms of the centre. He watched through the grimy glass panel on the door as Emily rested one of her legs on the back of a chair, gently stretching it out. She wore black leggings and a hot-pink top that came off at one shoulder, a low ponytail at the nape of her neck. Blake folded his arms and leaned back against the door frame, watching curiously as she tried out a few moves.

He was taken aback by the grace and confidence with which she moved, clearly reflecting some kind of professional training. He was also enraptured by the expression on her face, where all the tension and focus and sternness from earlier had melted away and her features were lit with joy, as though she was dancing in the grandest ballroom rather than in this shabby, cold centre.

He stood up straight as a few people trooped past him and opened the door with a bang, startling Emily out of her reverie. She stopped dancing and greeted the group enthusiastically, and he walked in behind them. Emily saw him enter and turned from the elderly lady she was chatting to.

'Everyone, this is our newest, um, volunteer, Blake.' She gestured at him and he looked around with a polite nod and a smile as a few more people filtered in. The group was comprised of mainly ladies and a few men, all at least seventy years old, bundled up in a variety of scarves and hats that they resolutely kept on as they sat down on the chairs Emily had laid out.

Emily stood before them in the middle of the room. 'Today we're going to be waltzing,' she said, to a murmur of delight from the group.

'Oh lovely,' one of the ladies said, clapping her gloved hands together, giving a muffled applause.

Emily put them into pairs and turned to Blake. 'Will you dance with Enid?' she asked, gesturing towards a lady perched on a chair, tiny and thin as a bird, who looked up at him with sparkling eager eyes.

'Of course,' he said gallantly, offering his hand to her.

She took his hand, her skin soft and papery underneath

his, and chuckled. 'Now don't go too fast for me,' she said with wink.

Blake grinned at her. 'I promise I won't.'

Emily showed the group the steps and they shuffled awkwardly around the room, moving as much as their winter coats and hip replacements would allow, except for Enid and Blake, who glided past everyone, in time with the music and in step with each other. The pace was a little slow for Blake, and Enid was, well, far too old and wizened to be his partner, but he did his best.

'You dance beautifully!' Enid exclaimed, looking up at him. Her hair was like unravelled cotton wool, gossamer soft tufts of pure white, and her eyes were bright, almost youthful, despite her clearly advanced age. Blake had never known his grandparents, but he imagined Enid was the type of grandma he would have liked to have; the sort of gentle, kind lady you saw on adverts and Hallmark films, who gave out sweets and undemanding smiles with never a strict word or a rule to enforce.

'You dance wonderfully yourself,' he said with a smile.

'I used to go to the dance halls when I was younger,' she said dreamily. 'Oh, the fun we would have, Betty, Percy, Julian and I.'

Emily watched them as they waltzed past, her mouth slightly open with clear surprise and delight. Blake gave her a wide smile as he swished past, feeling somewhat smug at his ability to keep surprising her when her expectations of him were obviously so low.

'That was wonderful, everyone!' Emily called out as the music ended, and she hurried to her laptop to put on another track.

'That was just perfect, but I think I need to sit down.

You've tired me out!' Enid said, laughing gently, and Blake helped her to a chair. She sat down with a small huff, resting her hands on her knees and taking a breath. 'But, oh please, you should dance with Emily.' Enid beckoned to Blake to come closer, and he leaned down, inclining his ear to hear the soft whisper of the old woman as she lowered her voice conspiratorially. 'She has such talent. I remember seeing her that one year on *Strictly Dancing with Celebs*, my favourite show. Goodness knows why she was only on one series and never came back.' Blake smiled, nodding politely at her senile ramblings. The poor old dear must be terribly confused to mistake Emily with a dancer from a TV programme.

Enid patted him on the shoulder, then spoke at a normal volume. 'Emily never has anyone to dance with properly here.'

'Thanks, Enid,' Emily said, with a slight frown at the comment. 'I have *plenty* of people to dance with, like Arthur,' she said, patting the arm of one of the men who stood near her, who was old enough to be her grandfather.

'I meant nice young men, like this one,' Enid said, gesturing at Blake and shaking her head. 'Go on, you two. Dance for us, please do,' she pleaded, clasping her hands together with a hopeful expression.

'Yes, yes, that would be lovely.' Arthur nodded and the rest of the group murmured their encouragement.

Emily looked across at Blake and raised her eyebrows. 'What do you say, Blake?' she asked.

He walked up to her and extended his hand. 'Gotta give the people what they want,' he said, looking around at the eager expressions that surrounded them – although he wasn't bothered about dancing with Emily, he was a little touched by how keenly these older people wanted to see them perform.

Emily nodded hesitantly and started the music on her laptop. She stood before him, and he placed one hand on her back and clasped her other hand with his. Blake kept his eyes level with hers, the waltz steps coming easily to him without hesitation. They moved smoothly around the room, allowing the rhythm of the music to sweep them along.

'How come you can dance so well?' Emily asked him quietly.

'I could ask you the same question,' Blake said. 'As for me, I had to learn ballroom dancing for a movie. Turns out I'm quite good at it.'

'Yes, you are,' Emily murmured, and Blake could hear the approving tone in her voice.

'What about you?' Blake found himself genuinely interested.

'I've always loved dancing.' Emily's eyes gleamed with what could have been wistfulness. 'I wanted to be a dancer when I was younger.'

Blake nodded and thought that a shadow of sadness crossed her face, just for a second, before it flitted away. Perhaps it was regret, he thought, at not being able to fulfil her dream and ending up teaching dance to pensioners in this run-down centre.

They carried on without talking further, and when the music ended, the group applauded them with gusto. Emily released Blake's hand quickly and turned to them. 'Come on, you lot. On your feet, it's your turn again!' she called out cheerfully.

Blake danced with the other ladies in the class, but

he found himself glancing at Emily over their shoulders, and almost wishing he could dance with her again. He had enjoyed it more than he'd expected – partly because all her earnest seriousness seemed to fall away when she was dancing, her manner softened and her eyes shone. He liked her more when she was dancing than when she was in full-on manager-mode, when there was a stressed tension to her mouth and eyes, and she seemed to be judging his every move.

When the class was over and the pensioners had filed out, he turned to Emily's laptop while she was putting the chairs to one side. He scrolled through the playlist till he found a track he wanted. He jabbed at the Play button, and she looked over curiously as he approached, hand outstretched.

'Show me your tango,' he said, and she raised an eyebrow, grinning at his challenge.

'I'm not sure you can handle it,' she said, her chin tilted up and her eyes flashing.

'Try me.'

✦ EMILY ✦

'Try me,' Blake said, staring intently at her.

Emily paused for a moment, wondering if she should take up Blake's challenge. She knew she needed to get back to work, but she didn't want to pass up the chance to dance with someone properly. She had so few opportunities to dance with a partner who knew his steps and who wasn't three times her age.

She walked up to Blake and took his hand as he tucked one arm behind her, drawing her close.

'Just try to keep up,' she murmured.

His mouth twitched in amusement. 'No problem.'

As they moved, he kept his eyes locked on hers, just the way it should be; no looking at his feet, no second guessing. Despite her best efforts, Emily found herself a little flushed from the depth of his gaze, for the first time really *looking* into those stormy eyes that she had only ever seen on the big screen before. He was a prick, of that she was sure, but he was also flawless, intense, captivating. She couldn't help but note the toned, lithe muscles under his shirt, the warmth of his hand on her, the scent of him – no doubt an expensive cologne – drifting to her as he flushed at the base of his neck and their pace quickened. As she hooked one leg deftly around him, Emily could understand why so many women found Blake Harris to be such a heartthrob. She smiled to herself as she realised that a lot of people would probably kill to be in her place right now.

Emily allowed the music to wash over her and pull her into the dance entirely, as it always used to when she was younger, and for a moment she could have been in the clubs of Buenos Aires, rather than in a freezing community centre. The music was driven by a fierce staccato rhythm, and their dance was both intense and playful at the same time. Emily loved the tango; it was a dance of power and passion, of impulse and improvisation. Blake seemed to be enjoying himself too, allowing her at times to take the lead, then surprising her with his own direction, wearing just the hint of a satisfied smile the whole time.

The dance ended and it took a few seconds after the music died for Emily to pull away, the music and the zeal she felt for dancing still coursing through her veins. She took a breath and pushed away a shuddering sense of regret that dancing was no longer something she could do professionally. She couldn't, wouldn't, allow herself to indulge that regret for even a second. She had made her choice, and as much as she missed dancing, she was trying to do the right thing by turning her back on it.

'That was good,' she said, hoping she didn't look too flustered. 'You're a great dancer.'

'You're not too bad yourself.' Blake appeared entirely unruffled, barely out of breath and as calm as stone. 'So … why didn't you do it?' he asked as she turned around to shut down her laptop.

'What?' she asked.

'Why didn't you become a dancer? You're obviously talented,' he said.

Emily coughed, uncomfortable with the question, although she felt a glimmer of pleasure at the compliment. 'It just didn't work out,' she said, waving a hand in the air dismissively. 'I, er, wanted to do something to really help people, like my family all do. Dancing just didn't really seem like the right course.'

Blake laughed. 'What?! That's a strange reason.'

'No, really,' Emily said, irked at his casual dismissal. 'My family are all high achievers, and have dedicated their time and their talents to serving others. I think that's pretty worthwhile, and I wanted to do something like them … something to make a difference.'

'But dancing helps people too.' Blake looked baffled. 'Art, culture, that's all important, it's part of the enrichment of human experience.'

'Well, I think I do more good working here than pursuing my own selfish dreams,' she said firmly, closing down the conversation, uninterested in Blake's opinions on her career. She had made her peace with her choices and didn't want to be questioned by someone who knew nothing about who she was and her motivations.

Blake shrugged. 'I think it's a shame, that's all. You have a talent which is wasted in here.'

Emily felt her throat tighten with frustration. She had put those dreams to bed years ago and didn't want anyone, let alone some arrogant, unrepentant actor, stoking them up again. 'I'm not wasting anything in here. I'm helping some of the most vulnerable in the community,' she insisted. 'And who are you to say? You know nothing about me, or my family.'

'So, what do they do, this great do-gooding family of yours?' he asked, his tone slightly goading now. He smirked as if he was enjoying her increasing irritation, and she could feel her cheeks flushing.

'My parents are in Africa running a number of UN projects, one of my brothers is a doctor working with them, the other is a top marine biologist dedicated to campaigns to clean up the world's oceans, another brother is the director of an international human rights organisation, and my sister is a barrister and campaigner for the rights of refugees.'

He raised his eyebrows, and she assumed he was impressed by her family's credentials. She knew she was – every time she mentioned them and their amazing achievements, she felt both a frisson of pride and a slight sense of inadequacy. Of course, Blake would be impressed too.

'Sounds like they *are* doing wonderful things for the world,' he said grudgingly. Then he looked at her, a scornful smile playing around the corners of his lips. 'And you're here. Teaching the waltz to pensioners.'

She sucked in a breath and clenched her fists at his mocking tone, feeling a surge of anger at his judgement of her. 'What have you ever done for others?' she hissed at him. 'And yeah, I may not be a high achiever like my family, but at least I'm trying and not living an entirely selfish, shallow, vapid life.'

Blake looked completely unconcerned by her comment on his lifestyle, and she felt that she should leave the room quickly, lest she was unable to remain professional. She grabbed her laptop and walked out of the hall without a backwards glance.

'You can go. You're done for today,' she called out over her shoulder as she slammed the door behind her.

Chapter Seven

Blake stuffed the duvet into the cover, cursing it under his breath for going so lumpy and misshapen. He couldn't seem to get it on right. He glanced over his shoulder at where Emily was standing, making a bed that was as perfect as any hotel bed he had ever slept on – the sheets tucked in tight, the duvet crease and clump free.

He sighed, scratching his head and wondering why the bed he'd made looked rather less inviting than the others that lined the hall. He made a half-hearted attempt to straighten it out, trying to look as though he cared, though he really couldn't be bothered.

He tensed as he heard Emily pass behind him, and her footsteps stopped as she looked coldly at his efforts. She put her hands on her hips and pursed her lips, clearing her throat.

'This could be a bit neater,' she said in clipped tones.

Blake flashed her an irritated glance. 'I don't see why it matters so much,' he said. 'Surely the night shelter guests will just be happy to be out of the cold and have a bed. Surely it doesn't have to be perfect?'

She drew her eyebrows down low and shook her head. 'Every year I pride myself on offering the best night shelter. I want people to really feel some comfort, to feel that they were worth having a big effort made for them. This could be their only chance to have something nice ...' she trailed off and bit her lip. 'Why am I bothering to explain this to you? I doubt you care,' she muttered gloomily.

Blake flinched. She was right, but her low opinion of him rankled like an irritating itch he couldn't scratch. He began theatrically thumping the duvet and pillows to remove the lumps, pounding in time to 'Last Christmas', which was playing over the radio. But no matter how hard he shook it, the cover wouldn't straighten out.

Eventually, it seemed that Emily couldn't help but take pity on him. 'Here, let me,' she said, reaching out and taking the duvet with a small smile at his dramatic display of bed-making. 'It's all twisted inside. No wonder you can't get this straight.' She shook her head. 'I'll show you a knack.'

She threw the cover off and turned it inside out, grabbing the duvet at both corners and turning the cover down over it, then doing it up at the bottom in a swift series of motions that left the duvet laying on top of the bed, neat as a pin.

'Easy!' she said triumphantly, turning to him with a smug look. 'I'm guessing you don't make the bed a lot.'

He looked at her sheepishly, slightly embarrassed that he couldn't do such a basic task. 'Um, I have housekeepers for that sort of thing,' he mumbled.

'Well, now you know how to do it, so can you crack on with the rest of them?' She swept her hand over the hall to indicate the remaining unmade beds. 'There are a few in the side room where we did the dance class – those need to be done too.'

'Sure thing.' Blake said, and the false enthusiasm in his tone only served to make him sound sarcastic.

He'd just managed to make another bed using Emily's technique when Darren sidled up to him. 'That looks better,' the young volunteer said, smiling shyly at him.

'Thanks. So, how many people are coming to stay tonight?' Blake asked as he began making the next bed while Darren positioned a portable heater near them, one of many puffing out meagre streams of heat, fighting a losing battle against the frigid air of the hall.

'I'm not sure, I think about fifteen tonight,' Darren said. 'I'm on shift so it'll be interesting; it's my first time doing the night shelter.'

'You're staying tonight?' Blake asked, impressed that a young man in his twenties, who probably had loads of better things to do, was going to spend a night volunteering with homeless people. It was pretty commendable, although Blake couldn't possibly imagine what Darren would get out of it.

'Yeah. We only host it once a week and this is the last week, so I wanted to do it before it finishes,' Darren said with a nod. His phone rang and he retrieved it from his pocket, frowning at the caller ID. 'Excuse me,' he said, walking away to answer it while Blake carried on working.

He only had a few more beds to complete, then he hoped he could go home and avoid any more boring tasks. He had already helped to unpack the grocery delivery, and then he'd cleaned the shower – an experience he would rather forget. All he wanted to do was go and enjoy his Friday night. It was tough to hit the London club circuit now he was sober, and it still felt way too dangerous to put himself into those tempting situations again, but he thought that he could at least go out to eat. He never had to worry about making a reservation, even at the most exclusive restaurants. The name Blake Harris still had enough gravitas to get him a table of his choosing, except for a handful of places where he was banned for a few nights that had got out of hand. He wished he still had a PA to book him a table and cursed himself for not having hired someone yet.

As much as he didn't want to admit it to himself, he didn't particularly want to stay at home that evening. He would just be on his own, wandering around empty rooms, wondering what was coming next in his life. For the first time in years, he had no major projects lined up, no marriage or divorces to celebrate, no alcohol to numb his mind. He pushed the thought away and focused on the beds.

Darren dashed back in, looking frantic and waving his phone at Emily from across the hall. 'Emily!' he yelled urgently.

Blake watched with interest as she turned around with an alarmed expression at Darren's panicked tone. 'What is it?!' she exclaimed.

'I'm so sorry but I've just got a call that my nan is really ill. I have to go … I'm sorry … I can't do tonight. I'm so *so* sorry!' Darren said, looking utterly wretched, his eyes glistening with barely suppressed tears.

'Oh Darren, that's okay. Please don't worry,' Emily said soothingly, patting him on the shoulder. 'Just go and be with your nan. I do hope she gets better.'

He gave her a swift hug. 'Thank you,' he said and hurried off, wiping his face roughly with the back of his hand.

Emily watched him go, a fretful look replacing her calm

expression as soon as he'd left. She whipped her phone out of her pocket and started dialling frantically.

'Hello, Fernando? It's Emily. I wonder if you can do me a huge favour …?'

Blake listened as she phoned volunteer after volunteer, none of whom could stand in at the last minute to do an overnight shift. They all had family responsibilities, work shifts, childcare issues. Eventually, Emily looked down, drumming her fingers on her lips, a frown creasing her forehead.

Blake looked at the duvet in his hand and had the sudden urge to throw it over himself to hide from her hopeful, seeking expression.

'Blake,' she said, smiling sweetly as she walked up to him. 'I don't suppose you can help tonight, can you?'

Blake coughed uncomfortably and readied a lie, but before he could respond, she carried on speaking. 'If I can't get an extra person to stay tonight, I won't be able to run the shelter. It won't be safe with just one member of the team overnight,' she said, her eyes wide.

Blake frowned. Of course he didn't want to stay there overnight; he couldn't think of anything worse. But then he looked at Emily's pleading expression and the tiny sliver of him that wasn't totally selfish – the small part of him that felt sorry for her – compelled him to open his mouth and speak before he could even think about what he was signing up to.

'Of course, Emily,' he said. 'I would be happy to help so that the night shelter can go ahead.'

After a moment in which she looked totally taken aback at his offer, her face lit up with a delighted expression. Blake puffed out his chest a little, feeling like a hero, the saviour of the night shelter. He had to admit it felt good to know that a bunch of homeless no-hopers would be spared a night on the streets just because he'd deigned to say yes. Now he just had to survive a night here.

How hard could it be?

✦ EMILY ✦

Emily stared outside into the night, the sky pitch black and starless, the streets lit only by the sickly orange glow of the streetlights overhead. She hovered in the doorway and waited for their first night shelter guests to arrive. Everything was ready, and although she had her doubts about Blake staying with her, the freezing rain and sleet that splashed over the pavement and ran deep in the gutter made her glad that they could go ahead. People were relying on them for a warm, dry place to stay, and that was the main priority.

The guests began to arrive and she ticked their names off the list with a smile, gesturing for them to go through to the hall and help themselves to hot drinks. Fernando had cooked up a storm earlier and the delicious smell of chilli sent warming wafts of paprika and spices into the air. The people arriving were all different ages and nationalities, but the rain had poured equally on them all, sparing no one from dripping coats and damp feet. Emily knew the hall wasn't the most comfortable or cosy of places to stay, but she could tell by the expressions on her guests' faces that it was a welcome refuge from the winter storm that pelted down outside and thrashed angrily against the windows.

She was relieved to have Gloria and Fernando helping

for the dinner service, even though they couldn't do the overnight shift, and she bustled around, serving and chatting, almost forgetting that in just an hour or so it would only be her and Blake left to supervise. When her mind did stray to that thought, she felt a sharp stab of anxiety, knowing that Blake wasn't like the other volunteers, who were trained and experienced and reliable. But she needed someone to make up the numbers and Blake was the only one who could.

She paused to have a drink and heard a loud eruption of laughter from one corner of the hall. She looked across to see Blake working his charm on a small group of the guests. One man in particular was laughing so hard that he was wheezing and began to sputter.

She walked up to them with a smile. 'Wilfred,' she said, handing him a glass of water. 'I've never seen you laugh so much.'

He coughed violently, doubling up with the effort, and Emily was worried to see how his hand shook as he raised the glass of water to his mouth. Suddenly his wheezing didn't sound like the result of laughter so much as illness.

'Are you okay?' she asked with concern.

Wilfred straightened up and grinned at her, even though he still looked pained from his coughing fit. 'It's this horrible British weather. When I was home in Jamaica, I had no problems with coughs or colds. But I feel okay, because this Blake, he is telling us some of his tales of Hollywood life.'

Blake leaned back in his chair and flashed her a wicked grin. 'I'm not sure you would want to know, Emily,' he said with a wink.

'Probably not.' She smiled and left them to it, glancing back at Wilfred, who still chuckled along with Blake's stories as he clutched his thin coat around him. She was worried about him, especially as he was one of the older clients and his health generally wasn't good. She didn't know his exact age, but she guessed he was around sixty. She made a mental note to check on him later and keep an eye on him.

It was gone 9 p.m. by the time they had cleared dinner. The guests were milling around, some watching the TV, others already laying down on their beds, including Wilfred, who seemed quieter and more worn out than usual. Emily told him to come to her if he needed anything, and she headed to the office, nursing a cup of tea. She sat at her desk and switched on a tiny heater, shivering slightly at the cold that seemed to permeate even the furniture in the room. She wrapped her hands tightly around her mug and looked up as Blake joined her.

He sat down with a sigh. 'Fernando and Gloria just left,' he said.

She nodded. 'It's just us two now till the volunteers arrive for the breakfast shift.'

They sat in awkward silence as Emily sipped her tea and Blake drummed his fingers on his knee. He glanced around and caught sight of a photograph on her desk.

'That's your family?' he said, pointing at it.

She nodded. 'Yes, my parents, three brothers and one sister.'

'Wow, five kids.' Blake whistled. 'That's a big family.'

Emily laughed and rolled her eyes. 'A big, crazy family,' she said, looking at the photo fondly. She felt a glimmer of sadness as she remembered how much she missed them and how long it had been since she had seen them all together.

'I hardly see them all,' she said. 'Most of them are abroad or travel frequently. My parents come back from time to time, but their lives really revolve around their African projects.'

Blake nodded and opened his mouth to speak, but her phone rang before he could say anything.

'Oh, sorry. I must get this,' she said, seeing River's name on the screen. She hurried out of the office and stood in the darkness of the entrance hall, enveloped in the cold air and wishing she had brought her coat with her. The storm was raging outside, the wind whistling through the power lines, and she shuddered at the sound of the wild weather.

'Hey,' she said softly as she answered her phone.

'Hiya,' River said cheerily. 'How's things with the night shelter?'

'Everything's fine here,' she said, glad to hear his voice. She hadn't spoken to him for a few days as they had both been busy, and she missed him. 'What are you up to?'

River cleared his throat. 'Well, um, I'm packing, actually.'

'Packing for what?' Emily asked, slightly alarmed.

'I'm going to Costa Rica tomorrow,' River said. 'I'm so sorry for the short notice Em, but an opportunity came up working with an animal sanctuary and it was too good to pass up.'

Emily gasped at the news, so unexpected and so unwelcome, and at the nonchalant tone that it was delivered in. 'You signed up to go to Costa Rica without talking to me first?' Emily couldn't help but be completely stung by the lack of consideration for her in his plans. 'How long will you be gone for?'

'Six months, maybe a little longer.'

Her mouth opened. She took a breath through her nose and tried to speak calmly, but she knew he would be able to hear the quavering disappointment in her voice. 'River, that's a long time. You could have told me you were thinking about going ... you could have asked what I thought.' She knew she and River weren't exactly on the cusp of marriage, but they had been dating a while; she'd been hopeful they might have been moving forwards.

'Well ... it's not like we're exclusive, is it?' River said, the laidback tone in his voice cutting Emily as much as his words.

'What?!' she exclaimed.

'I mean, you know, we're seeing other people, we're casual, so I didn't think—'

She interjected before he could finish. 'Hold on, you've been seeing other people?'

'Well, yeah. I thought you knew that?' he said, sounding utterly bemused.

Emily's mouth opened and closed in surprise and it took her a moment to reply. 'No. No, I didn't know,' she said firmly.

'Oh,' he responded.

She gave him a second to reply with something more comforting, something more constructive, but there was only silence down the line. She gripped her phone hard and clenched her other hand into a fist, wishing she had a stress ball, or maybe even a punch bag, nearby.

'You know what, River? Have a great time in Costa Rica with the turtles. And don't bother contacting me again.' She ended the call and rubbed angrily at the tears that had already escaped her eyes. She shook her head firmly, telling herself that she wouldn't waste a tear, nor another minute, on River.

She stormed back to the office where Blake looked up from his phone, seemingly amused at her furious expression.

'Boy trouble?' he said, grinning inanely, and she wanted to slap him almost as much as she wanted to throttle River.

Instead, she turned to her desk and shuffled some papers, trying to keep her thoughts occupied. 'No,' she snapped.

'I couldn't help but overhear,' he said.

She turned around. 'So what? If River wants to go to Costa Rica, he can go. Good riddance.'

Blake looked incredulous. 'River? Is that his real name?'

She shook her head. 'No. His real name is Barnaby.'

Blake burst out into peals of laughter, the sound making her jump. 'Barnaby?! No wonder he changed it.'

She couldn't help but crumple into giggles at his comment.

'So, the eco warrior has dumped you in favour of turtles, then?' he asked.

'I guess so.' She sat down and took a sip of her now-tepid tea.

'Don't stress about it, there's plenty more fish in the sea,' Blake said. 'Personally, I'm always on the lookout for the next Mrs Harris.'

Emily shot him a withering look. 'What'll that be? Number four?'

Blake nodded and grinned. 'That's right.'

'Were those other marriages just for show?' she asked curiously, wondering how he could be so unconcerned about three failed marriages.

'Oh no, not at the time. There were genuine infatuations,' he said, matter-of-factly, his arms folded behind his head. 'They just didn't last ... for various reasons.'

'That's a shame,' Emily remarked.

'Not really,' Blake said. 'It means I get an excuse for another amazing celebration the next time I get married. Weddings are fun.'

Emily closed her eyes for a moment and leaned back in her chair, feeling a fuzzy sense of tiredness seep through her muscles and envelop her brain. She wondered if Blake's glibness was genuine, and got the feeling that it wasn't, but who was she to judge? Clearly her love life wasn't exactly a resounding success either. She tried not to think about River's easy dismissal of their relationship, tried not to care about being single yet again, and hoped that the night would pass by without incident.

✦ BLAKE ✦

Blake glanced at Emily as she closed her eyes for a moment. She was clearly tired, and obviously hurt by the phone call he'd overheard. Her earlier bright enthusiasm for the night shelter had ebbed away, leaving her mouth downturned, and a slight smudge of mascara under her eyes hinted at tears she had roughly wiped away.

He felt a small pang of sympathy for her. Her boyfriend really shouldn't have called her to break up while she was at the night shelter. It was a pretty crappy thing to do.

Blake was no prize partner, but he wouldn't have done that, at least.

'You were telling me about your family?' he asked, changing the subject.

Emily opened her eyes and the tension around her mouth softened slightly as she smiled.

'They are pretty amazing,' she said, sounding wistful. 'They have achieved so much. When I think of the thousands of lives they've improved because of their work, I feel incredibly proud of them.' She paused and inclined her head towards him. '*Your* parents are, of course, incredibly well known.'

He nodded. 'Indeed. Hollywood royalty.'

'That must have been interesting, growing up with parents who were, *are*, so famous.'

He ran a hand over his chin. 'That's one way to put it – although I hardly ever saw them. I spent most of my childhood with nannies.'

'Oh,' Emily said softly. 'Still, what a lifestyle.'

He shrugged. 'I had everything I wanted, except my parents there.' He held up his hands, knowing that Emily would think he was just an over-privileged moaner. 'I know, I know, poor little rich boy, first world problems and all that. But every kid wants his parents, and mine were too busy so I hardly ever saw them. They never wanted me in the first place anyway.'

Emily raised her eyebrows in surprise at his last comment. 'How do you mean?'

'Well, they told me plenty of times that I was an accident. Mother never wanted children. They got lumbered with me and made the best of it, I guess.' Blake suddenly realised how much he had let his mouth run away with him, how much he had said that was private and should have remained so. He had spoken about such things before with his wives and friends and multiple therapists, but Emily was basically a stranger and he didn't know if he could trust her.

He smiled at her sheepishly. 'You know, it's best not to repeat what I just said, okay?' he asked hopefully.

She nodded. 'Don't worry. I'm not interested in selling gossip.'

'Well, you're in the minority. I swear I never know who I can tell anything to,' he said, thinking of one particular "friend" who had blackmailed him for a decent amount of money to keep his mouth shut over Blake's many indiscretions.

'That must be difficult.' She looked thoughtful, then she leaned across and turned up the small heater, though it didn't do much to fight the chill in the air. 'It's getting cold,' she commented, shivering a little and winding a long woollen scarf around her neck. The rain slammed into the office window with a steady drumming and she yanked the blind down.

'What do we do now?' Blake asked.

'Well, there's a spare bed in the hall if you want to go and have a kip,' Emily offered.

Blake thought of the unwashed bodies slumbering in the hall and suppressed a shudder. 'I think I'll stay awake in here, if that's okay with you?' he said politely. He was no stranger to staying up all night, and the next day was Saturday anyway.

'No problem.' They lapsed into silence, and she turned to her desk, reading through reports, while Blake scrolled through his Instagram feed, the newspaper gossip pages online, and then his emails. He glanced over at Emily, who was diligently typing on her computer.

'Do you ever stop working?' he asked.

She shook her head, the light from the screen making her look tired and drawn. 'Nope. Running this place takes a lot of time and effort and we don't have funding for enough staff, so a lot falls to me. I can't say that I'm particularly good at some of it, like the budgets and reporting. My siblings were always the smarter ones.' She added the last comment in a low mutter, sounding slightly deflated as she said it.

'You need a holiday,' he said. 'I hear Costa Rica is particularly nice ...'

She held up a hand to stop him. 'Enough,' she said, but there was a slight smile on her face.

They were interrupted by a hurried knock on the door and a man poked his head around, his eyes wide. Blake wracked his brains to remember the man's name, but he couldn't.

'Is everything okay?' Emily asked.

The man shook his head. 'I think Wilfred is ill,' he said, his face etched with concern. 'He said he had chest pains, then he went to the toilet and didn't come back so I went to check on him. I think he's in a bad way.'

Emily leapt to her feet and followed him out to the hallway, heading swiftly for the toilets. Blake followed them, curious to see what was happening.

Emily knocked gently on the door to the toilets and pushed it open. The harsh white beam of the fluorescent lighting spilled out into the dark hallway, and Blake could see Wilfred slumped against the wall by the sinks. Emily knelt down beside him, her face fraught with worry.

'Wilfred!' she said urgently, taking his hand and squeezing it. 'Can you hear me?'

He didn't respond. His eyes were closed and Blake could hear the shallow, agonised rasp of his breathing.

Emily looked up at Blake. 'Call an ambulance!' she cried, and Blake was chilled by the panic in her voice.

He whipped out his phone and dialled 999, relaying the address. He kneeled on the freezing lino floor beside Emily and felt Wilfred's cheek. 'He's so cold,' he said, taking off his jumper and wrapping it around him. Wilfred's normally dark skin was ashen, his lips tinged with blue, and Blake realised he could no longer hear the ragged breathing which had punctured the silence before.

Blake held a finger underneath Wilfred's nostrils, hoping to feel the movement of warm breath against his skin, but there was nothing.

Emily's hand trembled as she grabbed onto Blake's arm. 'Oh, oh … I should, I should, do … what should I do?' She turned to Blake, her eyes wide with panic, her hands now clutching at her cheeks, which had drained of colour.

Blake knew he had to do something. He lay Wilfred down on the floor and started chest compressions. He remembered every bit of the resuscitation scene in his last film and imagined that he was there again, letting his muscle memory take over, remembering the training he was given to make the scene realistic. He didn't even flinch when he covered Wilfred's mouth with his own, breathing hard into his lungs.

He focused on the chest compressions and the breathing and everything else around him faded away till he felt a hand on his shoulder, tugging him backwards; the green-clad arm of a paramedic telling him it was okay to stop, instructing him to stand clear so they could take over.

He looked up groggily, blinking, staggering away as Emily took his arm and gently pulled him out of the toilets into the hallway, where the blue flashing lights from the ambulance outside the entrance danced over their faces and reflected off the tin foil decorations swinging from the ceiling.

Blake ran a hand over his face and only then did the world refocus around him. He watched and Emily paced as the professionals took over, fitting an oxygen mask to Wilfred's face. The man appeared as light as a bag of old clothes as they gathered him onto a stretcher.

One of the paramedics patted Blake on the back as they passed by. 'He's breathing. Good job, man,' he said, doing a double take when he saw Blake's face, a flash of recognition lighting in his eyes. He opened his mouth as if to say more, but instead he turned and hurried off to the ambulance.

Emily leaned back against the wall, one hand on her chest and the other over her eyes. 'Oh goodness,' she said, and Blake could see she was trying to remain composed, but tears were tracking down her cheeks from underneath her fingers. 'Poor Wilfred. I hope he'll be okay.'

The guests had remained undisturbed and the man who alerted Emily had gone back to his bed, so only the two of them remained in the hallway.

Emily sniffed and ran her sleeve across her cheeks. 'I should have known what to do,' she said, shaking her head and looking at Blake. 'I'm first aid trained. I just … froze.' She looked at the floor. 'Useless,' she muttered, and her tears flowed faster.

'Hey.' Blake took one of her shoulders and gave her a small shake. 'It's fine. You did what you had to do, and it'll all be okay.' He tried to sound reassuring, but all he wanted at that moment was to clean his teeth, rinse his mouth out and sit down. He felt frozen and exhausted and his desire for a stiff drink prodded at him, prickling all over his skin like a thousand needles.

Emily looked at him. 'How did you know what to do?' she asked. 'You were like a doctor. No hesitation at all.'

'I played a doctor in my last film,' he said, feeling pleased at the admiring way she looked at him.

She nodded. 'You were amazing. I think you may have saved Wilfred's life.' She turned to go back to the office and he followed her back to the comforting glow of the heater.

'I hope so,' he said. He crossed his fingers for Wilfred and sat near the heater, wishing for a moment that his heroics had been captured on camera.

⋄ EMILY ⋄

Emily's mind was reeling as she started filling in the incident report forms. She tried to focus on the papers in front of her, but the adrenaline rush from the incident with Wilfred had left her nerves jangling and her hands shaking. She kept fidgeting and getting up to check the guests were all asleep and well, flinching at every unexpected sound.

She wished she could have gone with Wilfred, but she knew she had to stay at the shelter. Her thoughts returned to him every minute, her mind replaying his shallow breathing and his awful pallor. She squeezed her eyes shut and shuffled through papers on her desk, phoned the hospital, and all the while Blake Harris was sleeping in his chair, his head resting on his coat. She had no idea how he could have possibly drifted off after everything that had happened but his deep, even breaths told her that he was most definitely asleep.

When she returned from roaming around the hall for a third time, he sleepily opened one eye.

'Are you going to fidget all night long?' he asked wearily.

'I can't help it. I'm so anxious about Wilfred.' She bit her lip sadly. 'And so angry at myself for freezing up. If you hadn't been here ...' she trailed off, still unable to believe Blake Harris of all people was the hero of the evening. All that training she'd had, all the first aid courses and refresher days, all the times she had used those skills before, they had come to nothing that evening.

'You did great,' Blake murmured, not even trying to sound convincing. 'Don't worry about it.'

'I did not "do great",' she said snippily. 'I was about as useful as a chocolate teapot.'

He chuckled, his voice low and husky with tiredness.

'How can you be so relaxed after what happened?' she burst out. 'How can you possibly sit there and go to sleep?'

'Well, when you work long days on sets and party crazy hours at night, it's amazing how you can learn to sleep almost anywhere,' he said. 'And as for this evening, well, I just did what I remembered from my acting and that was it. End of.'

Emily stared at him, unable to understand his nonchalance, wondering if he had any emotions that ran deeper than a puddle.

'You're a strange man, Blake Harris,' she said finally, shaking her head.

'And you need to rest,' he said, leaning his head back onto his coat and closing his eyes once again.

Emily left him to sleep and paced around, hoping for news of Wilfred. The storm that raged outside finally began to calm, the howling wind dying down to nothing more than a murmur. She stood at the window and waited for dawn to come, which it did after what seemed like an endless night, creeping over the world weakly and without fanfare, as winter dawns do.

Chapter Eight

Blake woke to the welcoming smell of frying bacon. He sat up and immediately winced at the pain in his neck and the stiffness in his legs. He swore under his breath and rubbed his tense muscles, thinking that he would definitely need to book a massage that day.

As he unfurled himself from the chair, he took a deep breath of the welcoming aroma of breakfast. His stomach constricted with hunger and he realised that he was absolutely starving. He could hear the bustle and clatter of plates in the kitchen, and was just stretching with a deep yawn when Emily came in with a cup of coffee and a bacon roll. She handed it to him with a smile.

'Here,' she said. 'You deserve this, after what you did last night.'

He took them thankfully, and he was so tired and cold that even the instant coffee didn't taste too bad in that moment. He took a mouthful of the bacon roll and chewed enthusiastically.

'Delicious,' he said. 'Best catering in Lambeth.'

Emily grinned and sat down. 'Lizzie and a few volunteers are here for breakfast and to tidy up, so you're free to go whenever you want.'

He nodded. 'Sounds good.'

She leaned forward, an earnest expression on her face. 'Listen, thank you so much for last night. For volunteering at the last minute and for saving Wilfred. I can't thank you enough.' She gave him a warm smile, her hazel eyes glowing despite the dark circles around them.

Blake felt a glimmer of pride at her words. It felt pretty good to know that he had done something helpful, even though he was tired and stiff and hadn't been paid anything.

'You're welcome,' he said, smiling back at her.

Her phone beeped with a message and she turned away, checking it with a frown. 'Bugger,' she said with a tut.

'What's up?'

'Oh nothing,' she sighed. 'The storm last night must have dislodged some power lines near where I live. My neighbour just texted me to say the power's down on our road and it could be a good few hours before it comes back on.' She frowned, still scrolling through her phone.

'What are you going to do then?' Blake asked. 'Do you have somewhere else you can go?'

She bit her lip. 'I know Lizzie has plans today once she's done here, and my friend Tess is away at the moment. Of course, I would have gone to River's, but I guess he'll be on a plane by now.' She looked downcast then shook herself as if to disperse the negative emotions brought up by speaking about her ex. 'It's okay though. I can always stay here.'

Blake raised his eyebrows. 'And I bet you'll spend your Saturday tidying up and working, even though you've been up all night.'

She gave him a faint smile. 'There's always plenty to do.'

Blake's brain was fuzzy from lack of sleep and he was still basking in the glow of satisfaction about his good deeds the previous night, so the words tripped off his tongue before he had a chance to even think about them. 'You could come back to my place.'

She looked taken aback. 'Um, no, that's okay. I'm sure you have things planned for today.'

Blake shook his head. He couldn't withdraw the offer now, plus he did feel sorry for her. She looked exhausted, and he knew that she would only carry on working if she stayed here. 'It's fine. Honestly.'

She nodded slowly. 'Okay … that would be brilliant, thank you. I might just stay here a little bit as I can lock up after we're all done, but if my power hasn't come back on by then, perhaps I can come after that?'

He nodded. 'Sure, here's the address.' He scrawled it down on a post-it note he grabbed from the desk and handed it to Emily. 'I think I'll leave now,' he said, 'and maybe I'll see you later.'

'Sure.' Emily nodded. As he walked away towards the door, she called out after him. 'Blake?'

He turned expectantly, wondering if she'd changed her mind about letting him go and had decided to make him clean the toilet or do some other unpleasant task first.

'Thanks again,' she said, and Blake was surprised to feel another unexpected warm glow at having done something that didn't totally revolve around serving himself.

⇢ EMILY ⇠

Emily headed up the road, checking the directions on her phone. The street she was walking down was lined with what looked like normal homes, and she wasn't sure she was in the right place. There certainly didn't seem to be a mansion fit for a superstar actor anywhere nearby.

She carried on following Google Maps, hoping she was going the right way. The street surface glistened, slick and wet from the previous night's downpour, and her breath puffed out in small clouds as she drew her scarf closer around her neck. Her muscles felt sapped with exhaustion, and she shivered, unable to get warm as goosebumps rippled over her flesh.

She had been hoping that her electricity would have come back by the time she locked up the centre at 2 p.m., but her neighbour had let her know it was still out and she had no idea when it would return. She wished Lizzie had been free, or that Tess hadn't been away, but she didn't fancy going back to her house when it was freezing with no power. Blake was her best option for a warm place to wait, and she figured his home would probably be large enough for her to hang out in without getting in his way. She was lucky that her neighbour had a spare key and was extremely fond of Rocky, so she knew he would be looked after.

Her phone beeped with a message from Tess.

I can't believe you get to go to Blake's house! SO lucky. Tell me everything tomorrow.

Emily smiled and shook her head. She wasn't keen on intruding on Blake's life like this, and wasn't particularly happy to spend more time in his company. *But needs must*, she told herself, and she had to admit that she was a little curious to see how he lived.

Her phone bleeped and Google Maps told her that she had arrived at her destination. A huge pair of wooden gates loomed before her, and she pressed the intercom tentatively, looking into the camera.

'Hello? It's Emily,' she said.

She waited for a moment, then the gates cracked open and she marvelled at the driveway spread out before her. The path unfolded through lines of towering trees, a few with hardy golden leaves still clinging to them in spite of the fierceness of the previous night's weather. She walked for what felt like a mile, every footstep she took making her question her presence there even more as she drew near to the house, which looked more like a five-star hotel than a home. The huge property gleamed bright white even in the fading winter daylight, and she caught a glimpse of Richmond Hill rising behind it in the distance.

Blake greeted her at the front entrance. If she ignored his surroundings and his piercing looks, she could almost convince herself that he looked like a normal person, dressed in jeans and a maroon hoody, his dark hair swept back from his face.

'Your house is amazing,' she said, and he stood back to allow her inside. She gazed round the vast, snow-white atrium in awe. The furniture was a gentle dove-grey with an occasional splash of vibrant crimson on the cushions, curtains and lamps, and everything was pristine as if it had never been used. 'Wow!' she said, looking around. 'Just this entrance hall is bigger than the downstairs of my house.'

Blake grinned. 'It's a nice place. I'm only renting it though.'

'I would never have imagined a house like this was tucked away here on this street,' she said as she followed him to the kitchen, where white marble surfaces were studded with high-spec silver appliances. The room was dominated by an enormous fridge-freezer, the counters strewn with used protein shake packets.

'Lots of well-known people live around here. Tom

Hardy is just down the road,' Blake said with a nonchalant shrug. 'Do you want a drink?'

She nodded thankfully. 'Oh yes, a tea would be great.'

He snapped on the kettle and grabbed a mug. It was so strange, Emily thought, to see a Hollywood superstar here in his kitchen, making a mug of tea; something so normal conducted by someone whose life seemed anything but.

'Hey, I heard from the hospital before I left the centre,' she said. 'Wilfred has pneumonia. He has underlying health problems so it came on quickly and turned severe very fast, but he's going to be okay.'

Blake nodded as he handed her the tea. 'That's good news.'

'Thanks to you,' she said, taking a sip, grateful for the warmth of the mug on her hands, which were still icy from the cold outside.

Blake put his hands in his pockets and shrugged. 'Well ... I did my best.'

She hadn't quite expected him to be so humble about doing something so brilliant, but she didn't press it. She was more impressed by his humility than his designer clothes and his huge house.

'So, your power still isn't on then?' Blake asked.

She shook her head. 'Nope. My neighbour said it could be a few more hours. I hope it's okay that I came over. I tried to find someone else ...' she trailed off. 'No one was around today.'

Blake shook his head. 'It's fine. I didn't have anything planned.'

Emily found it hard to believe that a man like Blake didn't have plans, but she nodded. 'I don't want to get in the way if you need to go and do anything,' she said.

Blake smiled at her. 'Perhaps you'd like a tour though?'

She grinned with delight and put her unfinished tea down on the counter. 'I'd love to see more of the house!' He chuckled at her enthusiasm. She guessed for him houses like these were just normal, but she doubted she would ever set foot in such a nice place again, and she wanted to be a little bit nosey while she had the chance.

She followed him as he showed her the multiple living rooms, the nine bedrooms, the gym and the swimming pool. All the rooms were exquisitely and tastefully decorated, but none had any personal touches. There were no photos, no Christmas decorations. Most of the rooms had no personal effects in them, and a number were piled with unopened boxes. Emily wondered for a moment if they might be presents, waiting to be unwrapped by eager hands on Christmas Day, but they did just seem to be plain brown removal boxes with neat labels; not even a scrap of festively bright wrapping paper to be seen.

'How long have you been here?' she asked, expecting him to say a matter of weeks.

He thought for a moment. 'I don't know. A year or two, I think. I flit between places so I lose track.'

Emily was about to respond when he gestured for her to follow him into another room. She gasped as she walked through the door. 'Your own cinema! Do you watch your own films in here?' she asked jokingly.

'Ha! I never watch myself on screen if I can help it. Or my parents' films either, for that matter.' Blake snorted.

'They were pretty amazing in *Forever and a Day*,' Emily said, dreamily remembering the handsome Cole and his amazing chemistry with Mariella. It was one of her all-time favourite films; a classic romance that made her yearn for her own happy-ever-after.

'That's the film they met on,' Blake said, nodding. 'Where their great love affair started.' He muttered the last part with a slightly dark expression on his face.

'They still seem very much in love all these years later,' Emily said. 'I saw photos of them in the paper at a film premier the other night. I think it's very romantic how they've managed to stay together when so many celebrity couples seem to split after just a few years.' She didn't mean it to be a dig at Blake's own short-lived marriages and realised as she said the words that he might take it that way. She put a hand to her mouth. 'I mean, um, it's just a shame when things don't work out for some couples like they have done for your parents, that's all,' she clarified sheepishly.

Blake looked at her with a wry smile. 'Yes, they are very much in love. I was always a bit of a third wheel to their all-encompassing affection for each other.'

Emily frowned, finding it hard to believe even though he had mentioned it previously. 'Surely not?'

He shoved his hands in his pockets. 'Anyway, do you want to see the horses?' He had deftly changed the subject and his distraction had worked. She stared at him, wide-eyed with excitement.

'Wait, you have horses?!' she exclaimed.

'Sure,' he said, as if it was the most normal thing in the world. 'I bought two recently. I'm not a professional rider or anything. I just thought it might be nice.'

She smiled in amazement as she followed him through hallways towards the manicured gardens, studded with carefully managed topiary and ornamental features, then along winding paths towards the stables. The ground was hard under foot and peppered with snowflakes which had fallen while they were inside. Emily glanced up at the sky which hung flat and grey over them, like one enormous cloud without end, and wondered if a real snowfall might be on the way soon. It certainly felt as though it might be, and she pushed her hands into her pockets to keep them from the sharp edge of cold in the air.

Blake stopped in front of the stables and opened up the door. She followed him inside and took a deep breath of the warming scents of hay and leather. Blake led her to the first door. 'This is Trojan,' he said, as a jet-black horse poked his head eagerly out of the door. Blake rubbed his nose as the horse huffed gently at him. 'The other one is Honey,' he said, pointing to a gleaming chestnut mare in the stable next to Trojan.

'They're gorgeous,' Emily said, reaching out to stroke Honey, running her hands over the horse's mane and neck, and gently stroking the velvety-soft patch on her nose. 'Do you ride them much?'

'Sometimes,' Blake said. 'I used to ride a lot when I was younger and I saw these two for sale recently and bought them on a whim really. I was trying to recapture a happy memory, I suppose.'

Emily laughed softly. 'Most people buy new shoes on a whim, not horses,' she said, shaking her head in amusement.

'I guess.' He shrugged.

'You're so lucky.' Emily turned to Blake. 'If you want something you can just buy it. You can literally have anything you want in life.'

'Well,' he said, 'I suppose so. Although money can't

get you everything you want. All the money in the world wouldn't have helped my marriages to last.' His eyes didn't meet hers as he twined his hands around Trojan's jet-black mane.

'What happened?' Emily asked, genuinely curious.

Blake raised an eyebrow. 'If I tell you I have to get you to sign a non-disclosure agreement,' he said with a laugh.

'I'm not one for talking to journalists,' she promised softly, her tone serious despite his joke.

He hesitated and Emily was about to say he didn't have to tell her anything, that she was just being nosey, but he began speaking before she could.

'They just didn't work out. I was very young when I married Gabriella. I mean, eighteen years old! There was no way it would last. We were both too immature.' He shook his head, looking amused. 'Then, there was Adele. You know we met on the set of *Three Wishes*?'

Emily nodded. 'I heard.'

'I mean, she blew me away, I was completely besotted with her. And we did last three years, so I kind of call that a success.'

'Why did it end?' she asked.

'Well, there were some issues with cheating. I won't say who cheated on who, with whom,' he muttered darkly.

'Ah, right.' She nodded along as if she had any experience of marriage, which she didn't, and certainly wasn't any closer to having that now River had dumped her.

'And Anita, well, I was very infatuated with her,' he said matter-of-factly. 'But she found out about the whole … alcoholic thing, which I had kind of managed to cover up while we were dating. And her family hated me too. Literally, I think her dad wanted to destroy me.'

'But you went into rehab, right?' Emily asked.

'Yeah, but it was too little too late for Anita,' he said. 'She had already left me by then. And it took a good few stints in rehab to really help me get clean. The last one was after the hotel incident, but I had actually tried a few times before that.' He leaned back against the stable door and crossed his arms, staring at her while Trojan nudged the back of his head.

'It's a hard thing to do,' Emily murmured.

'Tell me about it,' he said.

They stood in silence for a moment, the only sound the gentle breathing of the horses.

'Let's head back, shall we?' Blake said abruptly, and she nodded. She was surprised by how much he had opened up to her and got the impression he felt he'd said too much. The cold air was permeating her clothes and prickling her skin, and she felt utterly spent from not having slept. She was sure she must look like a zombie to Blake, and as they walked back to the house, she hoped she could get some rest soon.

✦ BLAKE ✦

Blake led Emily to one of the many living rooms. It was his personal favourite, with huge windows overlooking the sweeping lawn, and buttery-soft leather sofas that were hard to get up from once you had sunk into their comforting depths. Emily stifled a yawn as they walked in.

'You must be exhausted,' he said. She shook her head, but he could see the dark shadows under her eyes. He had managed to have a little sleep at the centre, plus a decent nap before she came over, but she probably hadn't slept at all.

She wandered over to windows. 'I'm fine,' she said firmly. 'What a great view. Do you think you'll stay here long-term?'

'Nah. I get bored of being in one place too long,' he said. The truth was that nowhere ever felt like home to him. He was always moving on, never putting down deep roots. He'd bought various homes with his various wives when he'd been married, but those short-lived marriages had never compelled him to truly settle. He lived out of semi-unpacked boxes, in mansions that he rented or hotel suites he occupied. He never hung pictures on the wall, never chose a colour scheme and never picked out furniture.

Emily looked around from the window. 'Where are you going to put your Christmas tree? I bet you can fit an absolutely huge one in here.'

He snorted. 'No. I never decorate for Christmas.'

'What?!' she exclaimed, looking genuinely shocked. 'Why?'

'I just can't be bothered,' he said. Even though he told himself he didn't care, a small welt of bitterness smarted in his heart at how empty and boring his Christmas was going to be this year – no wife and no booze. 'It's not like I have a big family gathering here. Speaking of which, are your family coming back for Christmas?'

She shook her head. 'It's not likely. They like to spend Christmas overseeing their various projects, and it's tricky to get everyone together as they're all so busy and in different countries.' She said it lightly, but she couldn't hide the way her mouth dropped with sadness at the words.

'What do you do on Christmas Day then? Work?' He was joking but was taken aback when she nodded.

'It's not exactly work. We put on a huge Christmas buffet at the centre for people to drop in and help themselves. And we do a toy collection for poorer families in the area and take that round to houses on Christmas Eve. It's really nice, such a lovely atmosphere.' As she said it, her expression brightened. 'Even though my family aren't around, it's a wonderful way to spend Christmas. After all, it's a time for giving, isn't it?'

'And then?'

'Then what?' She looked blank.

'You go home and ...?' Blake pressed.

'Um, I watch TV,' she said with a faint smile.

'No wonder you prefer to be at work,' Blake said, shaking his head.

She frowned a little. 'Yeah? Well, what will you be doing this Christmas?' she asked, her tone slightly snippy.

'Oh, I don't do anything,' he said. 'I'll just treat it like any other day.'

'Why?' She looked completely baffled.

'That's the way I've always done it,' he said shortly. He didn't want to go into details about the real reason he didn't celebrate Christmas. He could remember exactly when Christmas lost its magic for him. He was seven years old and his father had told him he and his mother were off on a Christmas break and Blake would be left with the nanny. He had pleaded to go with them, but his mother had shaken her head with a sigh, telling him it was a child-free resort. If Blake lingered on the memory, which he tried not to, he could still feel the hurt and anger. He'd taken it out on his presents, throwing every single one out of the window, refusing to eat, and crying himself to sleep. He had sworn never to celebrate Christmas again, and his small, raging promise to himself was the only one he hadn't broken over the years, even when he'd been married, much to his wives' frustration. While they had picked out presents and celebrated with their families, he had skulked alone at home, booze in hand and bitterness in his heart.

'I really like this time of year,' Emily said softly as she took a seat on the sofa, curling up with her feet tucked under her. She gave a tired, wistful smile. 'I love everything about it – the cold weather, the Christmas songs, the bright lights, marshmallows on hot chocolate, ice skating outside the museums, all the brilliant, slushy, sentimental stuff that comes with it.'

'The weather?' Blake tutted. 'It's so gloomy and dark and cold all the time. And don't get me started on cheesy Christmas music and lights.' He made a disgusted face. 'It's all so ... tacky.'

She scowled at his cynicism. 'Maybe you should come to the centre and see what it means to people who have nothing.'

He shook his head with a wide smile. 'My community service finishes before then, I'm afraid.'

'And then you'll be back to your celebrity lifestyle,' she muttered.

'Too right.'

She gave him a look, and he couldn't be sure what it was. Disappointment, perhaps?

'Christmas is a wonderful time for second chances, for turning over a new leaf, for trying to be the best person you can be, for making amends for past mistakes,' she said quietly.

Blake smiled at what he saw as her childish, rose-tinted view of the commercial holiday. 'Since when have you ever needed to turn over a new leaf, Emily? I bet you've been doing charity work since you were old enough to walk and have never done anything bad enough to need to make amends for.' He laughed, and she bit her lip, blinking hard. For some reason his comment seemed to have upset her, but he couldn't work out why. She didn't reply, instead she just yawned once more.

'Can I get you a coffee?' Blake asked, his tone gentler this time, recognising that she must be extremely tired and probably bored of the conversation, and also remembering that she'd never finished her tea.

She nodded. 'That would be great, thanks. I just need a bit of a caffeine boost to get me through the rest of the afternoon till the power is back on at mine, then I can get out of your hair.'

Blake left her on the sofa to make her a coffee, but by the time he returned she was already asleep, slumped over the sofa arm, her breathing deep and heavy. He wondered for a moment if he should wake her, but he saw no harm in letting her rest there. He looked around for a blanket and gently placed it over her, shutting the door quietly and letting her sleep. He had some work to do anyway, he thought, as he dialled his agent's number, hoping that Emily would stay dead to the world and not overhear.

✦ EMILY ✦

Emily opened her eyes, feeling warm and groggy. It was dark, and her cheek brushed against a material that was nothing like her pillow. She stroked her fingers sleepily over it. Soft, supple leather. She frowned in confusion, turning over, stretching out carefully. She was on a sofa. Blake's sofa.

She had no idea what time it was, but it felt like night time. She looked over at the window, and through a small gap in the floor-length curtains she could see the sky, with a single glimmering star winking at her.

She yawned deeply, and her heavy eyes were already closing again. She felt utterly exhausted, her muscles sore and her brain foggy. There was no point getting up and leaving now, she reasoned. Not when it was so late and when she was so comfortable. She allowed herself to slip back into sleep; the deep, heavy slumber of the truly tired.

During the day Emily was always focused on her job, but whenever sleep finally found her, she danced in her dreams. She relived auditions, shows and triumphs, all behind closed eyes. She recalled her first standing ovation, aged seven, as she danced to the Nutcracker for her appreciative parents. She experienced the exhilaration of winning the junior Latin ballroom championships, with a dress the colour of fire. She danced the Lindy Hop at a local swing dance festival and, though she was drenched in sweat and gasping, she never wanted to stop, laughing in delight at the exuberance of the 20s' moves. She remembered learning to line dance on holiday in California with her friends, she and Tess wearing matching Stetsons and collapsing into giggles. She felt the thrill of auditioning for *Strictly*, performing the Paso Doble, fierce and powerful and confident as a bullfighter. And now there was a new memory to replay: her salsa with Blake, his touch still tingling on her skin.

As Emily rested, her slumbering mind re-ran these moments of the life she had left behind, but one that she still lived through her memories.

When she opened her eyes again, her vision was blurred with tears shed in the dark, and the star in the gap of the curtains had gone. The blackness of the sky had lightened to a dark sapphire, and dawn was nearly here.

She sat up and stretched out her arms with a long, satisfied sigh. It had been a long time since she'd had decent night's sleep of more than five or so hours. Partly because she tossed and turned at night worrying about work, and also because Rocky happened to have some rather annoying nocturnal habits which frequently woke her up.

While she hadn't intended to stay over at Blake's, she had clearly needed the rest. She ran a hand through her hair, teasing out a few knots, the curls falling messy and tousled around her shoulders, and wondered if Blake was up yet.

✦ BLAKE ✦

Blake had completely forgotten that Emily was still in his home until she came padding into the kitchen at 7 a.m. He sat at the kitchen counter, sipping a black coffee and feeling uncharacteristically optimistic. He had gone to bed early, worked out in the gym that morning, and was already showered and dressed. There was something to be said for the sober lifestyle. He certainly was more productive, and mornings no longer passed by in a sickened haze of retching and headaches and pain.

'Morning!' he said, laughing at her confused expression

as she blinked sleepily. 'You were so exhausted you must have slept all through the night.'

She rubbed her eyes and stifled a yawn. 'I'm so sorry. How embarrassing! I guess the exhaustion really caught up with me.' She looked at him sheepishly.

He shook his head. 'Don't worry about it. You must be starving. I've got some croissants if you want something to eat?' She hesitated and he knew she wanted to say yes. 'I'll warm them up while you shower if you like,' he offered, feeling like an excellent host. Perhaps this was the new him, he thought – sober, productive, taking in poor charity workers when their power was down.

She looked uncertain, nibbling on her lower lip. 'I should really get going.'

'Why? It's Sunday. You don't have to work today, right?' he said, and he realised that he actually wanted her to stay. He had no plans and seeing someone else in the morning, besides his own gloomy expression in the mirror, was refreshing. 'Stay and have some breakfast,' he said more insistently.

'Okay, sure, thank you.' She nodded, a thankful expression on her face.

'Great. I showed you around yesterday, so feel free to use any bathroom you like. They all have towels and stuff.'

'Okay, I won't be long.' Emily walked off while he heated the oven and put the croissants in. He and Adele used to share croissants in the morning, when they'd been married. He thought back to the times when they had stayed in bed all day, trying to chase away their hangovers with more alcohol, eating croissants dripping with butter, arguing and having sex, and then arguing again. Blake felt a sting of sadness at the memory of what it felt like to be in love, to be close with someone, even if he and Adele had been terrible for each other and neither of them had been faithful, and, ultimately, he couldn't be more glad that their rocky marriage had ended.

He sat nursing his coffee, trying not to muse on past mistakes and former loves. A light rain spattered on the windows, blown by a biting wind, and he shivered, cursing the dull English weather, thinking longingly of the LA sunshine. His skin rippled with goosebumps, the earlier heat from his workout now long gone, and he went to his bedroom to retrieve a jumper.

He took a sweater out of the walk-in wardrobe and pulled it on, hearing the hum of the shower. Emily had inadvertently chosen the bathroom in his bedroom, but he couldn't really blame her. It was the closest to the stairs and the room didn't look like it was his anyway. Like all the rooms in this house it looked untouched, thanks to his scrupulous cleaners. All his things were hidden away in a giant walk-in wardrobe, the few personal effects he had by the bed were ensconced in the bedside drawer. He had even neatly made the bed that morning, inspired by Emily's night shelter tutorial.

It struck him for a moment how sad it was that someone could come into his bedroom and see no discernible evidence that he slept there night after night – not that he ever slept particularly well. He was lost in that depressing thought when he realised the shower had turned off, and before he could leave Emily wandered out in a towel, the steam from the bathroom gently seeping into the air. She didn't immediately see him and he couldn't help but glance at her, taking in the sheen of water on her skin and the swell of her breasts tucked under the towel.

Her chocolate-brown curls were straight and dark with dampness, splayed over her shoulders.

He knew he shouldn't stand there watching like a pervert, so he cleared his throat, leaning slightly out of the walk-in wardrobe. Emily jumped with a shriek, turning round and clutching the towel.

'Oh! What are you doing there?!' she yelped.

He indicated the hoody. 'Sorry! This is my room. I just came to get a jumper,' he said.

She looked down uncomfortably, her arms folded across her chest. 'I'm sorry, I didn't know,' she stammered, her cheeks blazing.

'No problem,' he said, walking away, resisting the urge to cast one more glance back at her. She scurried back into the bathroom, a hot flush still on her cheeks.

Blake waited for her in the kitchen, finishing his coffee, allowing his mind to linger for just a few moments more on the image of Emily after the shower. He shook his head and told himself to refocus on something else. He was only human and she was attractive, but they were like chalk and cheese, and thinking about her in a sexual or romantic way was a waste of his mental energy. He put the croissants on a plate, the warm smell of their crisp pastry making his mouth water. He was rummaging in the fridge for butter when Emily walked in. He poked his head out of the fridge and wondered if he should apologise again for walking in on her. He opened his mouth to speak but she began before he could.

'I better get going,' she said, her tone cold and her arms crossed stiffly across her chest.

'Don't you want a croissant?' he asked, with a frown of confusion at her sudden change of manner.

'No, thank you. I really should leave.' Her words were brusque and clipped, and she marched towards the front door without saying anything further.

He slammed the fridge door and followed her. Perhaps she *was* pissed off that he'd walked in on her in the bedroom?

'Emily? Is something wrong?' he asked as she reached the front door and turned around to face him.

She paused in the doorway, letting the cold air blow in around them, robbing the hallway of warmth.

'You know what, Blake? I really thought I had misjudged you. I thought you cared for no one and nothing but yourself,' she said, her eyes scanning his. 'And you began to convince me that I was wrong, the way you volunteered at the shelter and saved Wilfred's life ...' She trailed off, shaking her head. 'But you're just what I thought you were. Nothing but a self-serving publicity seeker.' An angry flush rose on her neck as she stared at him, her eyes blazing.

He stared solemnly back at her, trying not to feel irritated at her self-righteousness. 'Where has this come from?' he asked, putting on his best poker-face.

'Check the headlines,' she said, giving him a withering look, and then she turned and walked away.

Blake watched her leave, the damp strands of her hair dancing in the fierce breeze, accompanied by a few swirling leaves. As she fell out of sight, he strolled back to the kitchen, grabbed his phone and checked his messages. As he expected, there was a slew of emails and voicemails from his agent.

'Excellent work on saving that guy's life, Blake,' Alice crowed in one voicemail. 'The headlines about it are fabulous.'

Blake scrolled through his emails, checking the links she had sent him and nodding with approval at the stories they had fed to the press, with some nice additional quotes from one of the paramedics who was on the scene.

He grinned with satisfaction, seeing the glowing comments on the news stories. It was a shame it had pissed Emily off that he had briefed the press, but it was worth it. After all, the story was true and he needed the good headlines. He felt a pang of guilt about not looping her in, but he told himself he would deal with her tomorrow. He helped himself to a croissant, staring at the ones he had warmed for Emily, and felt the empty silence of the house bear down on him. For a moment he wished she hadn't discovered his actions quite so early in the day, so at least he could have had some company, but he brushed the thought away and ate his breakfast alone.

Chapter Nine

Emily stomped away from the Harris house, hearing the whir of the gate shutting behind her. She wrapped her scarf roughly around her neck and buried her face in its woolly fibres even though they made her nose itch. The frozen air enveloped her, the wind snatching the warmth of the house away, but her anger at Blake had made her feel so flushed that she didn't even feel the cold.

Her phone rang, jolting her out of her frustrated thoughts. She was relieved to see Tess's number.

'Hey,' she said, keeping the phone tightly tucked to her face so the wind wouldn't howl over their conversation. 'Are you back from your night away?'

'Yes! I got back late last night,' Tess said.

Despite her anger at Blake, Emily smiled to hear Tess's voice. She was the only friend from her dancing days that she had kept in touch with. Tess was one of the few people who really knew her well, who had been there for her when she'd made the decision to give up dancing, who had supported her through so much. She was currently working in the West End in the theatre so they rarely had time to meet up, but they kept in touch as much as they could.

'How was Bath?' Emily asked.

'Gorgeous! But that's not what I want to talk about – I saw the news about Blake Harris's good deeds at your shelter.'

'Hmmm,' Emily said, her irritation spiking again at the mention of the news stories that had blindsided her that morning.

'You don't sound too pleased. Isn't it true? Did he save that guy's life?' Tess asked, a note of surprise in her voice.

Emily cleared her throat. 'Well, he did save Wilfred's life, that's true. I'm just frustrated that he leaked the story to the press without telling me, and probably without telling my manager, or Wilfred himself.' She sighed. 'He just wants good headlines, Tess. He doesn't seem to care about anyone or anything but himself. I told him that before I left his house this morning and—'

Tess interjected with a shriek of surprise. 'Wait, back up a second! You were at his house this morning? Why? What were you doing there so early?'

'I stayed overnight—' Emily began, and Tess squealed down the line, making Emily wince.

'You stayed at Blake's house! What was it like? Did you sleep with him?! Tell me everything!'

Emily couldn't help but laugh at her friend's hysterical tone. 'Calm down, it's really not that exciting. I went over there as my power was out and I had nowhere else to go.'

'So, you didn't sleep with him?' Tess sounded slightly disappointed.

'No!' Emily exclaimed. 'Of course not!'

'Why do you sound so shocked at the question? You're single now and he is …' Tess sighed dreamily. 'Come on, Emily, he is gorgeous, you must admit that. I mean, it's Blake Harris we're talking about here.'

Emily shrugged. 'I suppose. But like I said, he only cares about himself and his publicity.'

Tess was silent for a moment. 'What did he look like in the morning?' she asked with a giggle.

Emily rolled her eyes. 'He looked great, fresh from the gym and sexy as a rumba. There? Does that answer your question?'

Tess laughed and the line crackled slightly. Emily looked up and realised she was near to the station. 'Listen, I've got to go. I'm going to get on the train. I'll talk to you later, okay?'

'Sure,' Tess said. 'Feel free to come over and hang out today. You can help me decorate my tree.'

Emily hesitated. She would love to see her friend, but she also felt like she should check in with Rowan about the press that had come out that morning.

Tess sensed her reticence and guessed why. 'Emily, it's a Sunday. Don't go to work. You work way too hard. I know why you do it, but just cut yourself a little slack, please?'

Emily smiled at her friend's gentle cajoling. 'I'll see.'

'You know, I'm always being told about auditions for shows – there's a lot of work on at the moment because it's Christmas. People are always on the lookout for dancers ...' Tess trailed off.

'I have a job,' Emily said, wishing Tess hadn't brought up the career she had rejected and yet still yearned for deep down. She knew it was impossible to achieve her dancing dreams now.

'Sure, yes, of course,' Tess said. 'I was just saying, that's all.'

'Thanks, love. I better go. Hope to see you later, okay?'

'Bye!' Tess ended the call. Emily put her phone away and scrabbled in her pocket for her Oyster card. All she wanted to do was go home, change, eat and see her friend, but a worried guilty niggle, the one she always carried with her, prodded her in the back of her mind about work, about all there was to do. She shook her head, hoping to dislodge it for a little while, and walked through the barriers to her train, trying not to think about Blake or work.

When she got to her station, she realised how starving she was. Feeling shaky from lack of food, she quickly bought a bacon roll from a café, wolfing it down as she walked, wiping the ketchup from her chin. The high street was thronged with Christmas shoppers, seasonal tunes blasting from every door she passed. Even though the shops had only just opened that Sunday morning, people were already laden with bags.

Emily felt sad that she wasn't buying any gifts for her family, but she wasn't sure when she would be seeing any of them. She pondered what she would be buying them if they were here. She smiled as she thought of her childhood Christmases, which were so full of people and noise and squabbles and lots of food and hand-made gifts. As she thought of her family, she stopped suddenly and pulled out her phone, scrolling through her messages. She had forgotten that she was meant to Skype her parents today! She started jogging briskly towards her house, her cheeks and ears turning bright red with both the exertion and the cold wind that whipped past her face.

She ran up her road, nearly stumbling on the uneven pavement, and almost threw herself indoors in her haste. She made it home with just a few minutes to spare. Rocky sent out a series of alarmed squawks as she crashed in through the door and fumbled with her scarf.

'Hey, Rocky! It's only me!' she called out to her feathered friend. She walked to his cage, still breathing heavily, and he whistled happily to see her, bobbing his head.

'Hi, buddy,' she crooned. 'I hope Mavis took good care of you?' She was referring to her neighbour who had checked on him while the power was out. Emily made a mental note to buy her some chocolates as a thank you.

'Mavis!' the parrot crowed, then made a kissing sound.

'Wow, you really like her, huh?' Emily chuckled as Rocky nodded vigorously.

She checked her watch. 'Sorry sweetie, I've got a call with Mum and Dad.' As she turned to the dining room table to find her laptop, hidden under piles of papers and unopened letters, Rocky made a shrill ringing noise – the perfect imitation of a phone ringing.

'Not that type of call, Rocky – a Skype call!' she said, giggling at her parrot's antics while she opened the laptop.

'Emily, love!' her mum chimed when her parents appeared on the screen. 'So good to see you!'

Emily grinned at them fondly. She hadn't spoken to them for a few weeks and she was so glad to see them, both tanned a healthy nut-brown by the sun, wide smiles on their faces.

Her dad loomed into the camera. 'Hi, sweetheart,' Ralph said.

'Hi, beautiful!' Rocky screeched from his cage, craning his neck to see the computer screen.

Ralph leaned towards his camera, peering as if to see behind Emily. 'Good to hear that Rocky is still as loud as ever,' he said, looming into the screen.

'Dad, move away from the camera!' Emily laughed. 'I don't want to see up your nose.'

Rocky imitated a sneezing sound behind her and Emily collapsed into giggles. Ralph chuckled and sat back slightly.

'So, how are you, titch?' Linda said, her voice warm with affection.

Emily shook her head. 'I wish you wouldn't call me that anymore, Mum,' she said, rolling her eyes. 'But I'm fine, thanks. Very busy as usual at this time of year.'

Linda smiled. 'How're things at the centre?'

Emily nodded enthusiastically, trying to drive away the image of Blake which seemed to be haunting the edges of her mind whenever she thought about work – which was constantly, of course. 'It's good. We're getting ready for Christmas, which you know I love.' She paused and Rocky decided to fill her small silence by whistling the opening bar of 'Jingle Bells', to her parents' obvious delight. She waited till he had finished, and continued. 'How about you guys? Fill me in on what's been happening over there.'

Ralph nodded. 'Well, there's always so much to do.' He ran a hand through his hair, and Emily could see by the lines around his mouth and eyes that he was tired. Emily nodded along as her parents told her about the projects they had been working on. She listened, as she always did, with admiration for how they were able to oversee multiple projects, budgets and staff, all in a country which wasn't their own, whereas Emily constantly felt like she was drowning just trying to manage the one community centre. She wished she had their organisational skills.

'What about the others?' Emily said, referring to her siblings. 'Have you heard much from them recently?' Emily spoke with them from time to time, but she realised they had all been so wrapped up in work that she hadn't heard from her brothers and sister for a while now.

'Well, Caspar is always busy here with us, although he couldn't join in today as he's in the clinic with Annabelle,' Linda said. 'They're pioneering some new treatments here which will really make a difference when it comes to the malnutrition cases we're dealing with.'

Emily grinned with pride at her brother and sister-in-law's skills. 'That's wonderful!' she said. 'And the kids?'

Linda looked blissful at the mention of her grandchildren. 'Leo, Lucas and Leonore are absolutely thriving here. They're at a birthday party today, and oh Emily, they are getting so big.'

'They have so much energy!' Ralph chimed in.

'Oh, and Jack and Logan are spending Christmas with Jenny and Alejandro this year,' Linda said.

'That's so nice,' Emily murmured, slightly envious that her brother Jack and his partner would get to spend Christmas together at Jenny's home in Mexico.

'And Will and Daphne are so busy I can barely keep up with them at the moment,' Ralph said. 'They're in Geneva over Christmas I think, but you know Will – I doubt he'll take much time off.' Linda paused. 'You really should come and visit us soon, titch,' she said. 'The kids would love to see you too.'

Emily shook her head wistfully. 'I wish I could, but it's so hard to take time off as there's no one to really run things in my place,' she said, thinking longingly of her niece and nephews and how little she really knew them.

'You should be able to take a small break though, surely?' Ralph asked, and Emily laughed, somewhat bitterly. 'You're a fine one to talk, Dad,' she said.

'Seriously though, you look tired. Are you eating enough? Getting enough sleep?' Linda frowned at the camera.

Rocky made a loud snoring sound, and Linda's concerned frown melted away with amusement at their clever pet.

'Yes, Mum. I'm fine.' Emily rolled her eyes, knowing that her mum and dad worried about her more than the others.

'How's River?' Ralph asked brightly, and Emily winced. She hadn't told them about the break-up yet and she knew they'd been hopeful that River was "the one", especially as they'd loved him and his passion for the environment. They had met him just the once, when they were on a very brief visit back to the UK, but they had been bowled over by his energy and enthusiasm for all things environmental.

'Um ... we broke up,' Emily mumbled, wishing she had more positive news to report.

Linda's face fell. 'What! Why?'

Emily hesitated. She could tell her parents the sad truth, that River had been seeing other people and decided turtles in Costa Rica held a greater appeal than her, but it made her feel rubbish to say it.

'It was mutual,' she said finally.

'Oh no, Emily, we really liked him,' Linda murmured, looking disappointed. Emily hated to disappoint her parents, and she slumped a little in her chair, her mouth downturned.

Seeing his daughter's morose expression, Ralph interjected. 'But whatever works best for you, I'm sure you made the right decision,' he said, giving Linda a pointed glance.

Emily smiled faintly and nodded. 'Right.'

The screen flickered and her mum started to speak, but the picture stuttered and froze. Emily frowned and jabbed at the keys, but the connection dropped. She sighed and sent her mum a message. Her parents' Internet was always a bit sketchy, but at least they'd managed a short conversation; she was grateful for that at least.

'Bye bye,' Rocky crooned, and Emily looked around at him.

'Never mind, huh? We'll chat to them again soon,' she said. She never felt silly talking to a bird. Rocky had been theirs for so long, nearly twenty years, that he was like another member of the family. Emily smiled at him and he whistled softly back at her, and as ridiculous as it seemed, she thought she saw sympathy and sadness in his dark beady eyes as they regarded her.

Emily yearned for her family to be around for Christmas, but she was so proud of what they were achieving and knew they had way more important things going on. She only wished she had exciting news to tell, achievements to share with them, anything to make them proud and show them that, despite her past mistakes, she could be as good as they were. But all she had to tell them was that she had broken up with River. She shut her laptop and sat for a moment, but the impatient squawking of her feathered friend, demanding food, soon interrupted her gloomy thoughts.

✦ BLAKE ✦

Blake paused his frantic cycling on his exercise bike to gulp down some water. He felt the sweat drip down his back and cycled slowly, breathing hard, his lungs tight and his muscles burning. As his heart rate slowed down, he thought over the day and how surprisingly pleasant it had been having Emily at his house – until she had stormed off.

His mind lingered on the image of her after the shower, but then all he could see was her hurt and bemused expression as she discovered his briefing to the press. He did feel bad. He didn't want to undermine her, or take her by surprise. He just wanted some nice headlines for once, and the lifesaving he had done at the night shelter seemed too good to keep to himself. His agent and publicist had agreed. Emily, clearly, had not, but he would have to try to apologise to her tomorrow.

His phone rang loudly, interrupting his thoughts. He retrieved it from his pocket, sitting up straight on the exercise bike. It was his father calling.

'Blake, how are you doing?' Cole drawled as he answered the phone.

'Still on community service,' he said, knowing his parents had probably forgotten.

'You're still doing that? I bet you're desperate for it to end!' Cole laughed.

'You could say that,' Blake said, although it struck him that he actually wasn't so keen for his time at the centre to finish. He didn't have time to really think about why that was as his dad carried on talking with a cheery tone.

'Listen, we're going to Muscat for Christmas this year,' Cole said. 'We were wondering if you'd like to join us, seeing as you won't be spending it with Anita, obviously.'

Blake sighed. Now that he was an adult, his parents occasionally deigned to offer him the opportunity to spend Christmas with them on whatever exotic holiday they were on. He never accepted. He couldn't think of anything worse.

'No, thanks. I'll be fine,' he said curtly.

His father was clearly relieved by his refusal. 'Okay, I'm sure you have better plans anyway. Speaking of plans, we'd like to see you at the fundraiser this week.'

Blake scratched his head. 'What fundraiser?'

'You haven't forgotten, have you? We're throwing a little Christmas charity benefit at the Dorchester. Having the three of us there together will look good – you know – family-oriented.'

Blake resisted the urge to sigh. 'Oh yes, the fundraiser. I'll be there.'

He hung up the phone and grimaced at the idea of the benefit, at the false cheer, the way he would have to pretend to be part of a family, pretend to like Christmas, pretend to care, his engagement with all of it as fake as the snowflakes and glitter that would inevitably decorate the ballroom. He wouldn't even have a woman on his arm to accompany him.

He carried on cycling, pumping his legs hard, ignoring the need for a stiff drink that always rose when he felt stressed. He cycled on and on, refusing to think about alcohol, his parents, Christmas, or community service. He pushed through the pain barrier and felt endorphins sweep through him, leaving his muscles hot and trembling as the sweat dripped down his face. He already couldn't wait till Christmas was over.

+ EMILY +

Emily sipped her tea, eyeing up the Christmas tree in Tess's living room. Tess lived in a modern apartment block; a new build that was one of many that had sprung up, seemingly overnight, filling in the gaps of the London landscape with new towers of glass and steel.

Her place was in Battersea, not too far from Emily, but her home was as far removed from the tatty, jumbled semi that Emily occupied as you could get. Tess's apartment had as many toilets as bedrooms, and a brand-new kitchen with shiny black cupboards and pristine silver appliances.

The Christmas tree had built-in lights, Emily noted. *Very convenient.* 'No tangles,' she said out loud, and Tess shot her an amused look as she sat down.

'Your hair?' she asked. 'I doubt that.'

Emily laughed. 'The tree,' she said, nodding in its direction. 'No lights to untangle.'

'Right!' Tess laughed and folded her long legs beneath her onto the sofa.

'I thought you said I could help you decorate,' Emily pouted, upset that she had been robbed of the pleasure by Tess's already sparsely decorated, and very classy, tree.

'I would never let you decorate my tree. You have awful taste,' Tess said, matter-of-factly, whilst drinking a mouthful of hot chocolate. 'It was just a lure to get you here.'

Emily threw a cushion at her head. 'Hey!' she exclaimed, trying to look indignant, but her mouth belied her amusement. Tess was right, and Emily was grateful she had been persuaded to come and spend that Sunday evening with her friend rather than being at home, stewing about Blake.

'At least my trees have some colour on them,' Emily continued. Tess's tree was pure white with a silver sheen on the snowy needles. On every few branches there hung a glass bauble, frosted with white or pale blue glitter, or decorated with a silver ribbon. Everything matched, and it *was* pretty, Emily thought. Just not how she would have done it.

'I have to ask you about Blake,' Tess said, and held up a hand as Emily opened her mouth to protest. 'You didn't give me enough detail on the phone. I need more.' She wriggled to get comfortable, tucking one bare foot supply under her leg and pushing a strand of bright blonde hair behind one ear.

Emily gave an exaggerated sigh to show her unwillingness. 'Fine. What do you want to know?'

'What I really want to know is what he's like in bed?' Tess said with a wicked grin. Emily had always loved her friend's infectious grin – she had a big joyous smile that she was always happy to share, which infused her blue eyes with warmth. But, right now, Emily was unimpressed by it and gave Tess a withering look in response to her question.

'I can't tell you because I didn't sleep with him,' she said. 'You'll have to research that on your own, I'm afraid.'

Tess giggled in response. 'Believe me, I'd love to.'

Emily wrapped her fingers around her hot mug of tea and stared at it morosely. 'The annoying thing is, Tess, that I get it, I really do. I'm not blind. He's hot as hell. But he's just so ...' She grimaced, trying to find the words.

'... he pushes your buttons,' Tess noted, arching an eyebrow.

'He shouldn't have leaked that information to the press,' Emily huffed. She was still annoyed about the fact that he hadn't warned her, nor gone through the press office of the charity. The location of his community service hadn't been named, but guesses could be made, and she didn't know if Wilfred would be okay with the story being in the news, although his name was kept private. And on a personal level, she was terrified that somehow her name might come up, causing stories about her to resurface.

'I know you don't like the media,' Tess said softly, seemingly reading her mind and touching her on the arm. 'But come on, Emily. It *was* a true story, and a good one. Why wouldn't he want it in the papers?'

Emily rolled her eyes. 'I suppose,' she said grudgingly.

'So … did you get an insight into his lifestyle from his house? What's he like in the morning? Did he tell you any good gossip about Hollywood?' Tess asked eagerly, her eyes shining.

Emily paused and remembered the conversations they'd had; the things he'd told her about his ex-wives, and the things he'd said about his parents.

'Nope,' she said with a shrug. 'He's a closed book.'

Blake could blab about his good works, but Emily wasn't a gossip and wouldn't retaliate by telling his secrets. That wasn't her style.

Tess's face fell. 'What good are you?' She threw her hands in the air dramatically. 'You go to a Hollywood superstar's house, stay the night, and all you do is have an argument with him about headlines rather than try to get him into bed. I'll never understand you, Emily.'

Emily leant her head back and laughed softly. 'Tell me how the show is going,' she said, keen to change the subject.

'It's such hard work and so tiring. I mean, this is the first time off I've had in ages. But it's just such a buzz, you know? Well, yes, you *do* know.' Tess shot her a look. 'I love being up there, surrounded by music and dancers, and everything is in time and in step and the audience is roaring ...' Her eyes took on a faraway look, as though she were there on stage in that moment. 'The best feeling in the world.'

Emily nodded and took a big mouthful of tea. It was too hot and the scalding liquid ran down her throat, making her feel as though her insides were burning. Which they were, but more with jealousy than tea. Emily pushed away the uneasy, sickly envy that nestled in the pit of her stomach. She was proud of her friend and had no plans to revive her dance career herself, but she couldn't help but crave what Tess described. It was indeed the best feeling in the world; Emily knew it all too well, and she missed it.

She swallowed hard and smiled brightly. 'Oh Tess, I have to come and see it,' she said softly.

'You should!' Tess said, nodding vigorously. 'And you know, I think next year they'll be reopening auditions ...' she trailed off. She leaned across the sofa and took Emily's arm.

'Imagine it, being on stage together. Come on, Emily, think about it,' she said pleadingly.

Emily shook her head. 'No,' was all she managed to force out.

'But it would be so much fun, and I bet you could still do it with some intensive training. I would help you learn the steps—'

'No!' Emily said, interjecting more brusquely than she intended. 'Thanks, Tess – but no. I can't, I won't, and you know why so please don't make me go into this.' She hated the way her voice suddenly trembled, sounding plaintive and weak. Tess nodded quickly, accepting, and changed the subject, much to Emily's relief.

Chapter Ten

Blake jumped out of his car and slammed the door, telling himself that he only had a few more days to get through before he could leave this place as a distant, grimy memory.

'Have a good day, Mr Harris!' his driver called out to him, and Blake snorted derisively in response, in no mood for pleasantries and platitudes on this dark and cold Monday morning.

Blake walked in the open door, shuffling past people who were entering the drop-in. He had tried to make it on time, but the traffic had been awful. Darren greeted him enthusiastically, running up to him as he came in.

'Blake, hi! I saw the article yesterday. How amazing – you're a lifesaver!'

Blake smiled at the beaming young volunteer. 'Thanks. I hope your nan is okay?' he asked, and Darren looked delighted that he had remembered.

He nodded. 'She's better, thanks for asking. In a way though, I'm glad you were at the shelter on Friday rather than me. It sounds like Wilfred is only alive because of you.'

Blake glanced up to see Emily come out of the office. She had overheard Darren's words and looked across with a pained expression. Blake knew how much she had beaten herself up about Wilfred already and he didn't particularly want to rub salt in the wound, especially as she was so pissed off with him yesterday.

Blake shrugged. 'Well, Emily was there, and Wilfred is okay, so all's well that ends well.' He walked up to Emily and she gave him a frosty stare.

'Sorry I'm late,' he said, looking as contrite as he could. 'There was terrible traffic.'

She nodded and handed him the frayed old apron that he loathed. 'They need you in the kitchen,' she said curtly.

'I'm on it!' He knew the false cheer in his voice was not fooling Emily. He turned and walked to the kitchen. Everyone he passed wanted to pat him on the back for his part in helping Wilfred, which they had all read about in the news yesterday. Lizzie gave him a dazzling smile as she walked by.

'Good job at the night shelter, Blake!' she trilled as she bustled around with her clipboard.

Blake could feel Emily's stare burning into his back and he nodded at Lizzie, feeling irritated at how Emily's disapproval somehow affected him more than all the good headlines and the praise put together. He knew he shouldn't care that she was pissed off – after all, who was she to him? He plastered on a smile and served up dishes with as much enthusiasm as he could muster, trying to ignore the fact that her ire rankled him and he couldn't shake off how much that bothered him.

After he had served the meals, Fernando handed him a bowl. 'Go and eat,' he urged him.

Blake went into the hall and sat down next to a man hunched over his bowl, who was so focused on his food that he didn't give Blake so much as a glance as he sat down. It was only when the man finished eating and sat back with a sigh that Blake recognised him as Tony; the one who had thrown the chair at the craft session the previous week.

'You're Blake Harris,' Tony said, glancing sideways at him.

Blake nodded. 'That's me.'

Tony gave a crooked smile, his skin responding with multiple creases, though Blake didn't think he could be that old. He looked rough and worn, like being exposed to the harsh life on the streets was slowly eroding him.

'I saw one of your films once,' Tony said.

'Oh yeah? Which one?' Blake asked warily, unsure if he really wanted to get into a conversation with the man who had flipped out so suddenly last week.

'I can't remember the name. You were good though, really good.' Tony smiled at him, the skin around his eyes crinkling like tissue paper, dark gaps in his mouth where a number of teeth were missing.

'Thanks man, I appreciate that,' Blake said.

'You were at the craft session last week too, weren't you?' Tony asked. 'I was having such a bad day that day. I didn't behave too well.' He looked at the table, his hands kneading a napkin, and Blake couldn't help but notice the dirt under his fingernails.

Blake nodded. 'I remember.'

Tony rubbed his eyes. 'Sometimes I feel like booze is choking the life out of me.'

Blake looked at him, and despite all their differences, he knew what Tony was talking about. Addiction was like a death grip; once its clawed hand closed in on you, it would keep squeezing and squeezing till it felt like there was no escape.

'When did you start drinking?' he asked softly.

Tony looked up at the ceiling, thinking for a moment. 'When I left the armed forces, I was working as a prison officer ... but I had so many issues. PTSD, you know?'

Blake nodded again, urging him to continue. He couldn't even begin to imagine what it was like in the armed forces and what this brave man had been through.

'I wasn't coping well, and I started drinking. I didn't drink much at first, but it began to spiral, and my wife left me and took my son with her, and the house was repossessed.' Tony paused, his voice raspy, and swallowed hard. 'I lived in my car for a bit, but I sold it for money, and the money went on booze because it was the only thing that made the day seem bearable.'

That was something Blake was familiar with – the pleasant vodka-induced haze, the deadening of the nerves, the feeling that time which had dragged was passing by more freely, the sense that nothing mattered as much as it did when he was sober. Somehow alcohol made all your burdens feel light, momentarily at least. He knew those feelings all too well; still craved them now and then. He listened as Tony continued speaking.

'Before long I was on the street and I had lost everything.' Tony frowned. 'And I can't say they haven't tried to help. People have tried to help, but I'm just too weak. I haven't got the strength in me.' He rested his head on his hands then looked at Blake. Pain was written across his face. 'I haven't seen my son in years,' he said, his voice low from a throat tight with grief.

Blake felt a wave of shame rush over him at hearing Tony's story. There were so many people in the world who were worse off than him, and he had spent years bemoaning his own circumstances and taking it out on others.

Blake reached out and touched Tony's arm. He ignored the unwashed scent arising from both his skin and his clothes and leaned closer. 'Listen to me,' he said in a hushed voice, certain no one could hear them over the din of the hall. 'If you want to, you can break the habit. You would be surprised at what you can do, Tony. You're a strong man – think about all you've been through so far, and survived. You can survive this too.'

In that moment, sitting next to this broken man and finding a connection despite the differences in their lives, Blake felt a deep desire to see Tony succeed. It didn't matter about getting headlines or good photos for press. All of that felt unimportant. What mattered was the person before him: a person who truly deserved help, and someone he felt he actually *could* help.

'Do you want to go to rehab, Tony? I mean, really want to go?'

Tony gave him a look of weary resignation. 'I want to. But ... I don't know if I can hack it.'

'Let me tell you about the place I went to,' Blake said, leaning forward to rest his elbows on the table. 'And you can tell me if it sounds like a place you might want to try.'

◆ EMILY ◆

Emily hovered around the hall, keeping an eye on the volunteers and the clients. Occasionally, she glanced over at Blake and was surprised to see him and Tony still deep in conversation. It was the longest Tony had ever talked to anyone, she and Lizzie included, and *they'd* known him for years. She watched from a distance, unable to tell what they were talking about, curious to know what Blake was so animatedly describing.

As the drop-in closed, they showed no signs of moving. She approached and Blake saw her, giving her a very slight shake of the head. She held back, wondering what was going on, when Lizzie called her name.

'Emily, can you come to the office? It's Rowan on the phone.'

Emily went to the office with a sinking feeling, knowing that Rowan would be asking for the reports she hadn't quite managed to finish yet. By the time she'd ended the call, and persuaded him to give her another few days, Tony had left and Blake was shrugging on his coat, having helped to tidy and clean, and was on the verge of following Fernando out the door.

'Blake? A word please?' she asked, and he held back, waving goodbye to Fernando and Gloria.

She waited till the other volunteers had left then she turned to Blake. 'I saw you talking to Tony for quite a long time today.'

He nodded, a sombre expression on his face. 'We chatted for a while. He's had quite a rough time of it.'

'I'll say. Was he okay?' She was a little worried about what Blake might have talked to him about. Tony was a very vulnerable man, and she didn't want him getting caught up in Blake's publicity schemes.

'He was fine,' Blake said. 'We just talked a bit about his service in the forces, that kind of thing.'

She nodded slowly and tried to think of the best way to bring up the issue of the press that he had courted about the incident at the night shelter. Her anger from yesterday was dimmed by an exhausting day at the drop-in, but she was still annoyed at him and he needed to know his behaviour wasn't acceptable.

'Listen, Blake, those news reports about Wilfred and the night shelter—' she began firmly.

He held up his hands and interjected. 'I'm sorry.'

'What?' *Was Blake actually apologising?*

'I'm sorry. I should have cleared it with you first.' He looked at the floor and stubbed at the chipped wooden boards with his designer shoe. 'It was just nice to read something good about me in the papers for once.' He gave her a sweet, earnest look of genuine contrition.

Emily didn't quite know what to say. She had expected him to be more defensive, and instead he had apologised, not to mention spent the last couple of hours keeping a deeply troubled man company. She couldn't stay mad at him, as much as she wanted to, and she also couldn't help but feel that something in his manner had changed. There was a sincerity in his expression that she hadn't seen before, a warmth to his steely gaze that she was sure was new.

'Okay, well, thank you for your apology ... just please don't do that again,' she said finally. 'If there's going to be press about the project then please let me know first.'

He nodded, looking chagrined. 'Noted.'

'I'll see you tomorrow then,' she said softly.

He smiled and walked away leaving Emily completely confused. Blake Harris just kept on surprising her.

＊BLAKE＊

Blake stretched out in the car, feeling pretty pleased with himself. He had smoothed things over with Emily, but more importantly, he had done something he felt really proud of. He couldn't remember the last time he'd achieved something that had given him so much satisfaction. He searched his memories for the things that he was truly touched by – award nominations, amazing reviews – and wondered if perhaps helping Tony was even more rewarding, more important, than those career highlights?

He hadn't wanted to talk to Tony at first, remembering his outburst at the previous session, plus he smelt terrible. But a couple of the things Tony said had struck him, and he realised that beneath the unshaven bravado and cider-soaked exterior, the man was hurting badly, trying to cope with what life had thrown at him and finding it too tough.

Blake didn't know what it was like to live a life like Tony's, but he did know what it was like to use alcohol as a crutch to make it through the day. And he also knew what it was like to try to stop drinking and feel as though it was impossible, like climbing a slippery hill covered in mud where you always ended up sliding to the bottom, finding yourself lower than when you started.

The thought of Tony was in his mind as London sped past. He wondered where he was that evening, where he would sleep, if he would try rehab. Blake hoped so.

His mind flickered over the people he had met recently – Stuart, and Tony, and Wilfred – and he thought of their lives of struggle and pain and discontent, and he felt ashamed. Ashamed about how much he had in comparison to others, ashamed of how much he had abused it and taken it for granted, complained about it, and how he had never tried to help anyone or give back ... until today.

And for some reason, it was Emily's voice in his head

that he heard rather than his own; it was her praise and approval that he wanted and couldn't seem to get.

He checked the date on his phone. He was only a few days away from finishing at the project. He still had time to make a difference. After all, as Emily had said, it was a time for giving.

Chapter Eleven

Emily looked out of the window, biting her lip. The wind howled angrily, yet another winter storm sending sheeting rain violently against the glass.

She shuddered and set out a few chairs, hoping that some people might make it, though she knew that very few people, if any, would come to the dance class in this foul weather.

'Let me help you with that,' Blake said, walking into the hall and grabbing a chair. 'I've finished helping Fernando deep clean the kitchen,' he explained, 'so I'm free to assist with the dance class now.'

'Thanks.' She nodded appreciatively. She winced as a crack of lightning split the sky. 'I don't think anyone will make it though,' she said sadly.

The dance class was the highlight of her week. She knew it was a little selfish of her to run a session based on a personal passion of hers, but she had so few opportunities to dance. Waltzing about with a few seniors at the centre was the only chance she had, and she relished it and always looked forward to it.

She took a seat to wait for the participants and Blake did the same. She glanced at the clock. 'I *really* don't think anyone is coming,' she said mournfully.

'What shall we do?' Blake asked.

'Well, I have tonnes of work to get on with … although, there is one urgent task you might be able to help me with,' she said, a bright idea suddenly popping into her head.

'And that is ...?' Blake asked, raising an eyebrow warily.

'Decorating the tree!' Emily said triumphantly. She had been waiting for a spare moment and she could use an extra pair of hands to help her.

Blake looked unimpressed. 'Great,' he said flatly, sounding unenthusiastic.

'Come on, it'll be fun,' Emily said with a smile. 'Help me get it out from the cupboard.'

Blake followed her reluctantly as she went to the walk-in storage cupboard. It was crammed full of dusty, unhelpful items, the shelves lined with broken computer terminals, rusty tools and various boxes of left-over craft materials, but tucked into a corner was one of her favourite objects in the whole centre. The Christmas tree. The battered cardboard box that housed it belied the enchanting item that nestled inside, just waiting for its chance to shine each year.

'There it is!' she said, pointing at it and unable to hide the excitement in her voice.

Blake eyed the cardboard box incredulously.

'Okay, so it's fake and not that big,' Emily admitted. 'But once we get it all decorated, it'll look brilliant – trust me.'

'If you say so.' Blake shrugged and dragged the box out of the cupboard. Emily followed him with two large plastic bin bags which were full of decorations. Blake sneezed violently, having disturbed the thick dust inside the cupboard.

'Bless you!' Emily exclaimed as he sneezed for the second, third and fourth time.

He scowled and dumped the tree where she indicated,

and she eagerly opened the box, pulling out the stiff, bright green branches, fluffing them out and fitting them together. She didn't need instructions as she had put this tree together so many times before. Within minutes it was standing, bare and plasticky, shining under the hall lights. Emily didn't care how fake it looked. It would be the spirit and joy that she decorated it with that would make it truly special, and she knew she had enough Christmas spirit for the both of them.

Blake folded his arms. 'What now?'

'Ah-ha, now we need the decorations!' she said, and with a flourish she turned to the large plastic sacks she had dragged with her from the cupboard and dumped the contents over the floor. A medley of shiny baubles and moulting tinsel scattered around, and a tangled string of lights followed.

Blake looked at the knotted mess with obvious dismay. 'Please tell me you don't want me to untangle that,' he said, pointing at the lights.

Emily turned to him with a grin. 'It's either that or deep clean the bathroom, Blake. Your choice.' She had to suppress a laugh at his scowl.

'I thought Christmas was supposed to be a season for being nice to people.' He sighed.

'It is! And decorating a tree is a nice thing to do,' she said firmly.

He grabbed the string of lights and began teasing out the knots while Emily clicked on a Christmas playlist from her laptop.

Blake shot her a look, his piercing eyes looking flatly unamused.

'What? It drowns out the noise of the wind,' she said

with wide eyes, trying not to look too pleased as 'Winter Wonderland' came on. She sang softly under her breath as she unwound the tinsel and began draping it carefully over the bare branches, standing back to admire her work, then making tweaks before adding more decorations.

Blake worked on the string of lights, cursing under his breath. Emily surveyed her handiwork again and turned to Blake, watching him frown at the lights.

'Why don't you like Christmas?' she asked him. His statement on Saturday had been playing on her mind and she had been curious to ask him why.

'Hmm?' he responded, his focus on a large knot which he managed to free with a sigh.

'You said that you don't celebrate it,' she said. 'I was wondering why?'

Blake cleared his throat. 'I don't have good memories of Christmas as a child.'

'Really? Even with your parents and the money and the amazing presents you probably got?' She tried to keep her voice from sounding too incredulous.

He stopped trying to untangle the lights and looked up at her. 'Yes, really,' he said shortly, and she thought she detected a glimmer of hurt in his expression.

She was about to press further when he stood up and handed her the lights. 'Brilliant, thanks,' she said, and draped them over the tree. 'It's nearly done.'

'You think?' Blake laughed as he looked at the tree, now laden with decorations, every spare branch covered, every surface either red or gold or silver or blue, the green of the fake needles barely visible. 'I can see you've gone for the less is more look,' he said, smiling with genuine warmth, his surly expression brightening.

Emily plugged in the lights at the socket and ordered Blake to step back. 'Behold!' she said, flicking on the switch. The tree burst into light, a myriad of sparkles shining out, illuminating every colour and bouncing off every bauble. Emily clapped her hands in delight. 'Oh, it's beautiful,' she said dreamily.

'Remind me never to ask you for interior design tips – you clearly have no taste, and I think you might also be colourblind,' said Blake, but he was grinning at her.

She smiled. 'I love it. *Now* I feel Christmassy.'

'You didn't before, with all the music and crafts?' Blake laughed and shook his head.

'It wasn't the same without the tree.' She glanced at her watch. 'Given that the dance class isn't happening and we've done the tree, I guess you can go for today,' she told him, expecting him to turn and leave as soon as she'd said it.

He nodded slowly. 'Or ...?' he began to say.

'Or what?' she asked.

'Well, you wanted to teach a dance class. I'm here. Teach me.'

She thought he might be joking but his expression was surprisingly serious.

She laughed. 'You already know how to dance.'

'My salsa is terribly rusty though.' He smiled. 'Just the one?'

Emily hesitated. The nagging guilty voice in her head told her that she had already taken too much time to work on the tree, that she should go and get on with the budget, file the paperwork that was piling up on her desk that she had been putting off, and update Rowan on their monthly report. But the part of her that longed to dance, the part she so often told to be quiet, that part of her screamed 'Yes!' to Blake's request and to the lingering, intense look he gave her as he asked.

She turned to her laptop and put on a track, her fingers trembling with anticipation. 'Just the one,' she said with a nod, feeling a tremor of excitement at getting to dance, telling herself it was nothing to do with the fact that the dance would be with Blake.

She walked up to him and put a hand on his shoulder, her other clasping his. His fingers closed firmly over hers, his skin warm to the touch, despite the cool air in the hall.

'You know the basics?' she asked.

'Why don't you show me?' He arched an eyebrow, looking into her eyes. She tried to ignore the unwanted flutter that his stare provoked in her chest, averting her gaze from his slate-grey eyes.

'You have to loosen up,' she explained, daring to place a few fingertips gently on his hips. 'You can't be stiff when it comes to salsa.'

'Can't you?' he said, and she felt herself go bright red at his flirtatious tone, to her annoyance.

She cleared her throat and showed him the steps. 'See?' she said.

He nodded, concentrating. When he stared at his feet, she summoned the nerve to put a finger under his chin and tilt his head up, feeling the slight rasp of his stubble. 'Look up, at me,' she instructed, 'not at your feet.'

He smiled and met her eyes, their feet carrying on the steps, their bodies swaying closer. She knew he was probably lying about being rusty as his steps, although basic, were faultless.

He seamlessly twirled her round and brought her back

to him, taking the lead and drawing her near. Despite the freezing storm that raged outside, Emily felt warmth run through her, from the exertion or possibly the intensity of Blake's gaze – she couldn't tell, but a surprise jolt of longing shivered through her. She didn't want to find him attractive, but the proximity of him, the taut feel of his arm muscles wrapped around her, the way his hips swayed against hers, was making her head spin as much as the steps. She felt a yearning to just dance and let go of all the worry and anxiety and stress – the intense, breath-catching desire for Blake took her completely by surprise.

And then the memory swept through her, and suddenly she was back in the ballroom again. The crowd was cheering and the lights were hot as the cameras followed her and Kian. The faded wooden boards beneath her feet became the highly polished floor of the *Strictly* studio, swirling with lights. She could feel the swish of the sequinned dress around her thighs, remember looking into her partner's eyes and telling him to relax as he struggled with the rhythm of the salsa.

Emily forced herself back into the present and told herself to breathe. As she and Blake swirled around the hall, she was dizzy, not with the momentum but with the surge of emotions that washed over her, from the longing to dance with Blake, to the pleasure and pain of the memories of her previous career. She took a breath, summoning all her self-control, and broke off the dance, releasing her hand from his.

He looked at her quizzically. 'What's wrong?' he asked, breathing hard, a slight red flush on his neck and at the opening of his v-neck jumper.

'I should probably get back to work,' she said, taking another step away from him, hoping he couldn't see her trembling.

He waved a finger at her and tutted. 'All work and no play ...'

She gave him an uncertain smile and ignored how much her body was desperate to step back to him and continue, despite the memories it stirred up. 'No time for play,' she said, scooping up her laptop and practically running out of the hall.

'Thanks for the dance,' he called out after her, and despite everything in her screaming to return and complete it, she headed back to the office.

⋄ BLAKE ⋄

Blake remained standing in the hall, feeling the heat in his muscles seep away, watching Emily as she left abruptly. He had no idea why she'd broken off their dance. They were just warming up, and he knew from the gleam in her eyes and the flush on her cheeks that she was enjoying it – but then it was like she had been gone for a moment, her eyes distant, focused on something only she could see. He had no idea what – he was no mind reader – but whatever had been in her mind at that moment had made her end the dance. Blake found to his surprise that he had been left longing to continue, desperate to see where the dance led them.

Blake was used to being surrounded by women who threw themselves at him. He had flings with so many co-stars, the women on the best-dressed lists, women with designer clothes and whitened teeth and enhanced breasts, women who were sculpted and perfected and tweaked. But Emily was different to them. She was supple and smooth and beautiful in her own natural way, with those tumbling curls and big hazel eyes. When she wasn't looking serious and tense about her work, Blake had to admit that she was incredibly attractive. He wanted to continue dancing with her, wanted to continue pulling her close, to see what would happen if he could just break down the barriers she seemed to put up around herself, for reasons he didn't know.

The storm raged outside as he went to the kitchen for a glass of water, unsure what to do.

Fernando was bustling around, checking off lists of food for the week. 'Hey Blake, I'm just about to leave,' he said. 'You might want to check online – I think there are lots of transport delays because of the weather.' Then he laughed and shook his head. 'Of course, what am I saying? You don't take the Tube, do you?'

Blake grinned. 'I do sometimes, but not today. I've got a car waiting.'

'Well, get home safe,' Fernando said with a nod and a smile as he left.

Emily poked her head around the door. 'I thought I heard you in here. You should probably go. It's getting pretty wild out there.'

He followed her into the hallway. 'What about you?' he asked. 'Fernando said there are train delays.'

She took out her phone and checked, sucking in a breath as she saw the notifications from TFL.

'Oh no, my line is down!' She scrolled frantically, obviously searching for a different route.

'I have a car. I'll take you home,' Blake offered.

She looked up from her phone. 'I live in Streatham – it's not really in your direction.'

'So? It's not like I have to drive,' he said. 'Come on, before the weather gets worse.'

She nodded hesitantly. 'Okay, that would be wonderful.' She grabbed her bag and coat from the office, locking the door behind her. The wind whipped around them as she opened the front door to the centre, and they hurried to his waiting car.

'Dan, this is Emily. We're going to drop her off home,' Blake instructed.

Dan looked startled at his generous offer, tapping in the postcode for Emily's house with a knowing glance at Blake, which he ignored.

'This is kind of you. Thanks, Blake,' Emily said.

'No problem.' Blake felt pleased he could help. They sat in silence, watching the suburbs sliding by outside the window.

'You're almost finished,' Emily said, breaking the silence and glancing at him.

Blake nodded. 'I know. A few days to go.'

'I hope it's not been too awful,' Emily murmured.

'Not totally,' Blake said, smiling at her, a little surprised to find that he didn't have to lie – the experience hadn't been as terrible as he'd feared.

'This is it,' Emily said, as Dan pulled up outside her house. Blake stared at the 1930s semi as she squeezed out of the car door, holding it tight against the wind that threatened to throw it open.

'Thank you again for the lift,' she said as she turned to leave, strands of her hair dancing in the breeze.

'Wait, I drop you home and I *don't* get invited in?' he said with mock horror.

'Um, would you like to come in?' She looked slightly surprised.

'Sure!' He jumped eagerly out of the car. 'I'll be back in a bit, Dan,' he said over his shoulder, and the driver nodded.

'I'll be right here waiting,' he said cheerily, turning on the radio to hear an endless stream of Christmas tunes playing again and again.

Emily beckoned for Blake to follow her. In truth, he was curious to see Emily's house, and he wanted an excuse to spend a little more time with her, especially after she had ended their salsa so abruptly that morning. *And it was only fair*, he reasoned. She had seen his house. He wanted to see hers.

He followed her up the path where the weeds were growing up through the cracks in the stones. She opened the door and it protested with a creak, the green paint peeling and faded. Blake was a little surprised at how unkempt the front of the house looked, but he knew how much Emily worked and guessed she had no time for DIY or decorating projects.

She gestured for him to come inside and pointed him to the living room. 'Take a seat. Would you like a cup of tea?' she asked.

'Sure,' he said, not really paying attention to her question. He was distracted by the sheer amount of clutter scattered around the house. Every surface held a photograph or a certificate, or some kind of foreign artefact.

He walked past a display of wooden masks, a feathered

head piece, a boat carved from bamboo and various tapestries hanging up.

He sat on one of the sofas, which was sagging and worn but pleasantly comfortable, and glanced around at the photos crammed on to the walls, hiding much of the faded magnolia wallpaper underneath. There were graduation photos, clippings from newspapers, framed certificates; the proud clutter of a high-achieving, philanthropic family. The display of graduation photos captured his interest and he walked over to look at the pictures. Most of Emily's siblings had multiple photos there, with a variety of gowns and hats, Blake assumed because they had both undergraduate and master's degrees, maybe even a doctorate or two between them. Emily's face was notably missing from that section of the wall.

She walked in with two mugs and he swung round quickly, not wanting to seem nosey. His arm brushed against the large Christmas tree that teetered in the bay window, its branches overladen with baubles and tinsel, in typical Emily fashion. He noted that this tree was somewhat lopsided, with a few branches missing, a slight brown tinge to its needles. It looked as though it had seen better days.

'Thanks.' He took the mug. 'What's with the tree?' he asked.

'Um, it's nearly Christmas?' she said, looking baffled.

'No, I mean it looks a bit worse for wear. What did you do to it?'

'Oh, I bought it from a garden centre. It was kind of left to the side, and I, um, well this will sound a bit silly, but I felt sorry for it.'

Blake laughed. 'You even have charity for Christmas

trees? Only you, Emily.' He felt a wave of fondness for her strange ways. In his circles, he was surrounded by perfectionists; only the best would do. It was refreshing to meet someone who prized the things in life that were less than perfect, who saw the value in something slightly damaged.

She giggled with him and curled up in one of the armchairs, her fingers absentmindedly picking at a small piece of the stuffing that was poking through the seams.

'It's better to have a lopsided tree than having nothing at all,' she said pointedly – a remark he chose to ignore.

'Are these all photos of your siblings and parents?' he asked, looking around at the photos again.

She nodded with a beaming smile that indicated her pride and affection for her family. 'I'll show you,' she said, standing up and pointing them all out. 'My mum and dad. Caspar, Jack, Will, Jenny. Those are Caspar's children: Leo, Lucas and Leonore. I don't get to see them that often, which is such a shame.' She sighed, running her fingers gently over the picture of the three children, their faces glowing from the sunshine, their blonde hair ruffled.

'Are all your siblings married?' Blake asked.

'Well, Caspar and Will are.' She nodded. 'Jack isn't married to Logan, and they are perfectly happy like that, and Jenny doesn't like the institution of marriage, although I can't see her and Alejandro ever breaking up. They've been together for years, solid as a rock.'

'And you're the youngest?'

'Yeah, by six years. A happy accident, my mum always said.' Emily smiled and Blake knew that, even though they were both accidental conceptions, Emily hadn't been made to feel like a mistake.

'I bet it was fun growing up with lots of siblings,' Blake said, and he couldn't stop the note of envy from creeping into his voice.

'It was always hectic,' Emily said with a nod. 'There were always people here, so much noise, never any privacy, and it was always utterly impossible to get in the bathroom.' She laughed.

'This house is kind of small for that many people,' Blake said. 'What is it, three bedrooms?'

Emily nodded. 'We shared. Jenny and I shared one room, the three boys had the other.'

Blake grimaced. 'Sounds cosy.'

'It was fun, although we fought a lot too.' Emily rolled her eyes, but Blake could see the gleam in them; the pleasurable glow given by joyful family memories. 'It's funny, all those years growing up here and I often felt so desperate for a little bit of peace and quiet, but now it's just me, I find myself wishing for that noise and chaos again, especially at this time of year.' Her smile dimmed slightly, then she looked across at him. 'I can't imagine what it must be like, being an only child,' she said. 'Did your parents want any more kids?'

Blake laughed harshly. 'No way. They didn't even want me, let alone any more.'

'Oh, I'm sure that's not true,' Emily said softly.

'Wanna bet? They told me so often enough,' Blake said grimly. He still struggled to forgive his parents for being so callously open about their lack of desire to have children. Their relationship was a lot easier now he was grown up and they seemed to take an interest in him as a person, but he always felt like a separate entity to them; a lonely moon orbiting the blazing star of their beautiful relationship.

'They actually told you that outright? I know you mentioned that before when we were at your house, but I just can't believe ...' Emily's forehead furrowed. 'I mean, I know it's not my place to say, but that's pretty awful.'

Blake nodded. 'My mother never wanted kids. She thought it would ruin her career, plus she was never particularly maternal. I always had everything I wanted though – they bought me the world. They just couldn't ... parent me.' He held up his hands. 'I'm sure you're thinking that I shouldn't feel sorry for myself, that there are lots of people who have it worse than I do.'

'Actually, Blake, no I wasn't,' Emily said insistently, leaning towards him, her face open and sympathetic. 'That's not a nice thing to hear regardless of what circumstances you grow up in. That must have been really hard.'

Blake was taken aback at the way her eyes softened with sympathy as she spoke, at the genuine empathy in her tone. He thought she would be harsher, or tell him he was lucky compared to most, but not even the tiniest flicker of judgement crossed her face.

'Is that why you don't really do Christmas?' she asked, slightly hesitantly.

He nodded slowly, sipping his tea. 'This time of year never felt that special to me. Maybe if I had my own family I would change my mind. I always thought if I could find the right woman, then it would make up for the lack of family feeling. But I haven't ...'

'... yet!' Emily interjected, with a smile. 'You'll find someone.'

He smiled at her sweetness and was about to respond,

but they were interrupted by a piercing whistle and Blake almost spilled his tea.

'The fire alarm!' he exclaimed, getting ready to move, knowing that the old Christmas tree was the perfect kindling and would go up in flames in a second. He reasoned they would have to act fast if they wanted to survive and he leapt from his chair, his muscles tensed and ready to flee.

✦ EMILY ✦

Emily couldn't help but laugh at Blake's shocked face.

'No, it's not a fire alarm, don't panic!' she said, putting a hand on his arm. 'It's just Rocky.'

Blake frowned in confusion, still looking ready to run. 'Um, what?' he asked, and she beckoned to him to follow her to the back room where she pointed at the cage in the corner. Another piercing whistle came from it, and Rocky hopped up and down, clearly pleased with his perfect imitation of a fire alarm. He energetically bobbed his head and tapped his claws against his perch, almost like he was trying to do the Charleston.

'Rocky. My African Grey parrot. Well, my parents' parrot,' she said, grinning. 'He must have heard us speaking and felt left out so he decided to scare us.'

'Parrots can feel left out?' Blake asked and followed her to the cage, where Rocky rubbed his head against the bars as they approached.

'Hello, Rocky,' she crooned. 'This is Blake.'

'Blake!' Rocky crowed.

Blake looked at her in amazement. 'He can talk! That's so cool.'

'Oh, that's nothing,' she said proudly. 'Rocky, sing for us, would you?'

Rocky began to warble like a soprano opera singer, walking up and down his perch as if giving a virtuoso performance, his chest puffed out.

Blake began to shake with laugher and Rocky fed off his reaction, bobbing his head and whistling, jolly as a postman.

'He's brilliant,' he said, wiping tears from his eyes. Emily was pleased with Blake's reaction to her beloved pet. She adored Rocky but she had invited people over before who had found him annoying. She was glad that Blake liked him – not that it really mattered, as he was unlikely to visit her again, but still … she was delighted that Rocky entertained him.

She stuck a finger through the bar and stroked Rocky's head, ruffling the soft feathers.

'I'm lucky to have him. My parents didn't want to leave him here, but they couldn't take him with them. Thank goodness really, otherwise …'

She trailed off and Blake prompted her. 'Otherwise what?'

'Well, otherwise the house would feel a bit lonely,' she said, hating how pathetic that sounded. She was always busy with work, she had friends, and, up until last week, she'd had River in her life – but the house, which had always been such an epicentre of noise and activity, felt empty and would feel more so without Rocky there.

'So, while your parents are away, you look after the house for them?' he asked.

'Yes,' she said. 'I don't mind, really. They have their work and it's so important. And it means I get to stay here rent free, and rents in London are insane.'

He nodded, looking unconvinced. 'But you could be in a flat share with friends. Or off travelling with River?' he said with a slight smirk. She glared at him and he looked contrite. 'Sorry.'

She shrugged. 'This arrangement works for me,' she said, although she did sometimes wonder if sharing a flat with other people would be more fun and certainly a lot less lonely.

They walked back to the living room to finish their tea, leaving Rocky happily humming behind them. Blake followed her but then abruptly stopped before one of the alcoves in the back room. 'Wait, Emily, what's all this?' he said, a note of surprise in his voice.

She winced. She'd been hoping he wouldn't see what was in the alcove.

'Oh, that's nothing,' she said, dismissively, hoping he would come back to the living room.

'Look at all these medals you've won,' he said admiringly. 'Programmes from theatre shows you've been in, awards, newspaper reports ...' he trailed off. 'Wait! You were on *Strictly Dancing with Celebs*? – so Enid isn't senile after all.' He turned to look at her, his mouth slightly agape with shock.

She nodded. She wanted to remove all the memorabilia, but her parents had insisted it stayed there. She was desperate to get rid of it all, but at the same time she couldn't quite bring herself to disturb it; it would mean being forced to look at the medals and the reports and the awards as she put them into boxes. It was easier to ignore it all and pretend it was nothing to do with her.

'No, she's not. But that was years ago, and I was only in it for a few weeks anyway. I'm amazed she recognised me but, then again, Enid is a super-fan of the show.' She sighed. 'Anyway, it's all ancient history,' she murmured.

Blake nodded, squinting at the dates on the clippings about *Strictly*. 'These were what, seven years ago? When you were …?'

'Twenty,' she said.

He frowned. 'Why did you stop dancing? I mean, you were on the biggest dancing show on TV so you must have been pretty good. What happened?'

She shook her head, the lump forming in her throat making it hard to speak. She swallowed hard and plastered on a fake smile. 'I just had a change of career, that's all,' she said brightly. She knew from his expression he didn't believe her, but she turned and quickly walked away to the living room, refusing to look any longer at the alcove that contained the few remaining fragments of her dreams.

'Your tea is getting cold,' she called out, and she was thankful that he followed her and didn't ask her again about her dancing, because she didn't want to talk about it with anyone, let alone Blake Harris.

Chapter Twelve

Emily walked up the street towards the centre, taking a deep appreciative gulp of the morning air. The weather had finally cleared from the storm and the pale blue sky was cloudless. The straw-coloured sun wasn't strong enough to chase away the freezing cold, but Emily loved the crispness in the air; a day without rain to look forward to if the forecast was right. The problems on her Tube line from yesterday's storm had been resolved, and she walked up the street at a leisurely pace, breathing in the warming scent of coffee and bacon from the local café.

To her surprise, Blake was waiting for her at the centre, bright and early at 8.45 a.m. – the first time he hadn't been late. He was lounging against the main doors, hands in his pockets, sunglasses on and a baseball cap pulled low on his head. His car was parked nearby, Dan waiting patiently at the wheel as always. He looked like any normal person waiting for the centre to open, and, of the people passing by on the street, only Emily knew that a Hollywood heart throb was hidden under the navy cap.

Blake grinned when he saw her approaching. 'Morning,' he said.

'You're early,' she responded, feeling an unexpected glow of pleasure at seeing him there. She put this down to him being on time for once, rather than the genuine way he was smiling at her, looking so pleased to see her.

'I just can't keep away.' He laughed.

She unlocked the doors and they entered, flicking on the lights.

'It's nearly your last day,' she said lightly as she shrugged off her coat and hung it in the office.

'It's gone fast.' Blake nodded.

Emily wondered if he felt any sadness at all that his time at the centre was coming to an end, or if he was just pleased that he had made it through his community service. She couldn't tell from his expression, but she hoped that he might feel a little downcast that his time with them was drawing to a close.

'What's on today?' he asked.

'It's our final craft session before Christmas, to finish all the decorations.'

'Do you want me to set up in the hall for you?' he offered, and she was taken aback at his easy enthusiasm. 'I remember where you keep all the materials.'

She nodded. 'Thank you, that would be brilliant. It'll give me some time to work on some other things.'

He walked off into the hall and she could hear chairs and tables being arranged.

She logged on to her computer, shaking her head in amazement at Blake's change of attitude. As her computer stuttered to life, Lizzie hurried in, bringing a cold blast of air with her.

'Morning!' she trilled, taking off her scarf and gloves and flinging them onto her chair.

'How's things, Em?' she asked, setting down her reusable coffee cup on her desk.

Emily nodded. 'Good, I think. Blake is setting up for the craft session.'

Lizzie raised her eyebrows. 'It seems like he's really

come a long way. I wonder why?' She glanced sideways at Emily.

Emily shrugged. 'I have no idea. What have you got on today?'

'A few keyworking meetings with clients. I'll probably meet one or two in the café, so I'll be in and out all day,' Lizzie said.

Emily nodded. 'Anything to update?'

'Actually, yes.' Lizzie frowned slightly. 'Have you seen Tony?'

Emily thought back to when she had seen him last. It was at the drop-in two days ago, when he'd been talking to Blake. 'On Monday,' she said. 'Why?'

'It's probably nothing. It's just that the street team from St Mungo's usually see him in his usual spot every night and they haven't for two nights. They were asking after him.'

Emily frowned, feeling a stab of concern. Tony was a creature of habit – when he was on the streets, he could be found in the same place each night. Like most people who slept rough, he had spots that he favoured; ones which were dryer, or more sheltered, or safer. 'I wonder where he might be,' she said softly. 'Perhaps he got into a hostel?'

Lizzie shrugged. 'If he did get a place it wasn't arranged by us or by St Mungo's,' she said. 'I hope we see him soon.'

Emily nodded and watched Lizzie walk off. She sighed and turned back to her emails, of which there had been a flurry yesterday. There was never enough time to keep up with the mountain of paperwork, and the number of unread messages flashing in her inbox and on her voicemail sometimes gave her nightmares.

She scrolled through a few and checked her watch.

9.30 a.m. It was time to open for the craft session, and she'd barely made a dent in any work. She got up, went to the door and, to her surprise, found a small group already waiting eagerly. There were additional people who didn't normally come to the craft session – Pavel, Stuart, and, to her delight, a person she hadn't expected to see there at all.

'Wilfred!' she exclaimed. 'How are you?'

He grinned at her. 'I'm better, thank you – thanks to your super volunteer.' He chuckled softly. The grey tinge to his skin had disappeared, and he looked worn but healthier than when she had last seen him. 'I'm on antibiotics and I'm very tired, but I wanted to come today to see Blake.'

'I'm so glad you're better,' she murmured, her heart filled with joy to see Wilfred smiling. 'And Stuart and Pavel, how nice to see you both,' she said, turning to them.

'I hear Blake is helping with crafts, so I also want to help with crafts,' Pavel said in his usual sombre way.

She smiled and stood aside to let them all troop in. 'You're all so welcome,' she said. 'Thanks for coming.'

She was so pleased at the turnout, especially as it was their last chance to make more decorations. Although they didn't sell for much, their sale would still help to raise a modest sum; every pound and penny made a difference.

Blake stood up as they entered the hall and welcomed them warmly. 'Wilfred!' he said, shaking his hand firmly. 'It's great to see you.'

'All thanks to you my man,' Wilfred said. 'I owe you my life.'

Blake shook his head. 'I just did what I could.' He was surprisingly humble, and Emily watched with amazement as he got Wilfred seated, joked with Linda, courteously offered Bella a hot drink and greeted Johnny with enthusiasm. He quickly got stuck into conversation with Stuart about his job prospects and showed Pavel how to make a bauble.

Emily watched him for a moment, wondering where the taciturn, selfish, moody Blake had gone. She just couldn't work him out. She turned to Linda with a smile and began to help with the decorations, trying to focus on the crafts rather than Blake's jovial conversation with Wilfred and his kind encouragement of Stuart. She couldn't believe the optimism and cheer she saw shining through on Stuart's face; a man she knew was struggling so much to keep things afloat. She had to blink hard against the tears that sprung to her eyes as the sweet sound of Judy Garland singing 'Have Yourself a Merry Little Christmas' filled the hall, and she wondered if she was witnessing some kind of Dickensian miracle turnaround, like that of Ebenezer Scrooge.

'I love the tree, Emily,' Linda said, pointing at the tree she and Blake had decorated a few days ago.

Emily nodded. 'Thanks, Linda. I can't take all the credit though – Blake helped.'

Linda smiled warmly. 'What a wonderful job you both did.'

Bella turned to look at it. 'It's beautiful – so bright, so festive.' She turned to Blake. 'What a good job you have done here. I wish you could stay for longer.'

Blake smiled and glanced at Emily, and she found herself thinking the same thing. She mentally shook the thought away, knowing she was just being sentimental because of the Christmas music filling the air.

She allowed the craft session to run on longer than usual, as the group were so enthusiastic and it was their last one of the year. Eventually, though, she had to close up, and they filtered out reluctantly, saying warm goodbyes to Blake. Emily returned to the hall after closing the doors to find Blake packing everything away and sweeping the floor. She stared with delight at the boxes of decorations they had completed that day.

'Look how many there are,' she said, marvelling at the amount – more than they had ever made before. 'I do hope we can sell them all.'

Blake looked over. 'I'm sure they'll sell,' he said encouragingly. He had removed his jumper and was sweeping in his T-shirt. Emily looked at the tattoos curling over the tanned skin of his forearms. She tried not to stare at the muscles she could see, defined and firm underneath the thin cotton. Blake ran his hands through his hair to sweep it back, and Emily found herself wondering what it would be like to run her fingers through it.

She mentally shook herself, remembering how much work she had to do. There was no time to stand and gaze at Blake, whose new sweetness was making him even more attractive. 'Um, I have to go to the office and sort out a few messages, if you can clean up here?' she asked, and he turned and nodded.

'No problem.'

She headed back to the office to make a decent go of her inbox. She lost herself in reports and emails and messages, feeling like she was making some headway, skipping lunch and forgetting Blake was still around. He found her at the end of the day, still staring doggedly at her screen, her eyes dry and her fingers numb. The funding reports had been coming in and were dismal. She wasn't sure what was going to happen to the centre, although she hoped she could find a solution – either way, she knew another late night of work was in store, despite her best efforts to finish at a reasonable hour.

'Ahem,' Blake coughed and rapped on the door, breaking her concentration.

'Hey! I'm so sorry, I totally forgot you were here!' she said, turning around. 'What have you been up to?'

He smiled. 'Lizzie found me and asked me to help her with a client and some computer work, so I was doing that most of the afternoon.'

'Oh, thank you so much!' Emily said, relieved he had been kept busy. 'I guess I'll see you tomorrow.' She turned back to her screen, blinking several times and rubbing her eyes to try to moisten them.

Blake remained, hovering in the doorway and shuffling his feet awkwardly. 'Hey, listen, I have something to ask you.' He paused and cleared his throat. 'My parents are throwing a charity benefit, in one of the ballrooms at the Dorchester, before they go back to LA. It's tonight.'

She nodded. 'That's nice. What's it in aid of?'

He paused, shaking his head with a frown. 'I have no idea. Trees? Owls? Dolphins? Something environmental I think.'

Emily couldn't help but laugh at his disinterest. 'I didn't think you or your parents were really into charities and fundraisers,' she said.

'Well, they do this one thing a year. I think it's for tax break purposes or a favour they owe someone possibly,' Blake said with a shrug.

'Okay, I hope it goes well,' Emily said and turned back

to her computer screen, wondering why he was telling her about his parents' faux philanthropy.

'Do you want to come?' He said the words in a rush, and she looked back at him, startled by the invitation and not sure she had heard correctly.

'What?' she asked.

'Would you like to come?' he said, more slowly.

'To the benefit?' she asked incredulously. 'At the Dorchester?'

'Yeah.' He nodded. Seeing her hesitate, he carried on quickly. 'Look, it's probably boring as hell and I'm obliged to go but I thought, because it's a charity-related thing, you might be interested.'

Emily paused. It was an opportunity to meet people with money who could be potential donors, plus she so rarely got invited to fancy places, let alone one of London's top hotels. Plus, she would get to rub shoulders with the wealthy and the famous, including Cole and Mariella Harris. She knew she couldn't pass up the opportunity, no matter how much work she had to do.

'Okay, I'll go,' she said a little hesitantly.

'Don't sound so enthusiastic.' Blake looked a bit put out, and she realised she hadn't come across as particularly excited in her response to his unexpected invitation.

'I mean, I'd love to go, and thank you for asking. It's really kind of you.' She smiled more genuinely this time.

His expression brightened. 'Be at the Dorchester at 8 p.m.,' he said. 'I'll put your name on the guest list.'

She nodded, caught up in the thought of going to the posh hotel as she watched him leave. She decided to tell Tess her exciting news and sent her friend a quick text.

Tess's response came back almost immediately, strewn with emojis and exclamation marks.

OMG!!! AMAZING!!! What the hell are you going to wear?!

Emily sat bolt upright in a sudden flash of panic. She hadn't even thought about that! Her pulse quickened to a foxtrot pace, and she tapped out a message to Tess, her hands shaking.

I need a favour!

✦ BLAKE ✦

'Absolutely marvellous creatures, don't you think?'

Blake nodded mutely and sipped his lemonade, as the man next to him wittered on about rhinos. Blake didn't care for the lumbering, ugly animals, and the conversation was boring him to tears. He couldn't understand why his parents had gotten roped into helping a foundation focused on rhinos of all creatures. They weren't even cute or cuddly.

He zoned out the ramblings of the other man and glanced around the ballroom, which glimmered with Christmas lights. At least it was tasteful for this time of year, but he would expect nothing less from the Dorchester. He spotted people he recognised amongst the attendees. His parents had made good on their promise to support the foundation by rounding up their famous friends. Singer Kiara Jacobs breezed past, a whirlwind of fiery hair and shimmering Dior, and gave him a friendly wave. He spied actress Katerina Murphy in a corner, deep in conversation and looking enthused, and in the midst of it all were his parents, holding court, laughing, glowing and chattering away as the Christmas lights shimmered overhead.

'Blake?' he heard an uncertain voice behind him and

turned around, sighing, preparing to make small talk with another dull philanthropist. But, instead, he was delighted to see that it was Emily standing there. She greeted him with a smile, looking slightly awkward as she shuffled her feet. Her golden gown draped gracefully over one shoulder and clasped tightly around her waist, cascading to the floor in a curtain of chiffon that floated gently along with her when she moved. Her hair was loose for once and tumbled over her shoulders, longer than he expected; a curtain of chestnut-coloured curls. Her eyes stood out even more than usual, gleaming in the low light of the ballroom and defined with a delicate sweep of black eyeliner. Her full lips shone with just a hint of crimson, as though warm from a fresh kiss.

'Woah.' He couldn't hide his surprise or his admiration as he gave her a lingering look, unable to tear his eyes away from her. 'You look ... amazing.'

She smiled at him, a tinge of pink in her face showing her pleasure at the compliment. 'Thanks. It's my friend's,' she said, gently touching the gown as if afraid to claim it as hers for the night, even though it fit her like a dream.

'Do you want a drink?' he asked.

She nodded and selected a glass of orange juice from what was on offer at the bar.

'They have Prosecco if you prefer?' Blake said, indicating the glasses, but she shook her head.

'No. This is fine, thanks.' She sipped her drink. 'This is so beautiful,' she said, eyeing up the glimmering lights and the decorations of the ballroom.

Blake rolled his eyes. 'If you like that kind of thing.'

'Well, I do,' she said firmly. 'You have to admit it's impressive! Don't be such a grouch.'

He laughed at her rebuke of him and nodded. 'I guess you're right.'

'Blake!' He heard his mother call his name. She approached, giggling, arm in arm with his father. Blake was always struck by how dazzling his parents seemed at events like these. They drew the eye of everyone in the room; his mother in a floor-length couture Chanel gown and his father in a tuxedo. But it wasn't just their clothes or their good looks that made them so appealing to all around them. It was the way they looked at each other, as if there were no one else in the world. Blake knew that look excluded him, and he simultaneously resented it, admired it and craved it for himself with a partner of his own who he still couldn't seem to find.

'I need you for a minute, darling,' Mariella said. She glanced at Emily with a smile. 'Who is this?' she asked.

Emily immediately flushed bright pink, and Blake was amused to see the unflappable manager fangirl over his mother.

'Emily, from the community centre,' he said. 'Emily, these are my parents – Mariella and Cole.'

Emily shook their hands with a shy smile. 'Nice to meet you,' she said.

His mother turned back to him. 'Please come and talk to Nicholas Stone. He has wonderful ideas for a film project and wants to involve you.' She leaned in close. 'Look, if you agree to at least look over the details, without committing, he'll be more amenable this evening.'

Blake nodded. 'Duty calls,' he said to Emily, feeling unwilling to leave her. 'I'll be back.'

He walked off and spent thirty minutes in conversation with the up-and-coming director, although it seemed like much longer, and he was glad when the guy was momentarily distracted and he could make his escape. Blake made his way through the crowd of people to search for Emily, realising she was the only one in the entire room that he actually wanted to speak to. Eventually, he found her, jabbering about the community centre to a large man who was nodding politely with a glazed look in his eye.

'So, you see,' she said earnestly, waving her glass of orange juice around, 'we're really a vital place for the community, and if we don't get the funding—'

Blake interrupted. 'Emily, sorry, can I borrow you?' he said, steering her away firmly by the arm.

'Hey! I think I was really getting somewhere,' she said indignantly, pulling her arm back from his grasp.

He shook his head. 'I don't think so. That's Miles Cleaver and he isn't interested in charity, trust me.'

'Oh,' she said, looking disappointed. 'But maybe for this—'

'Nope!' Blake interrupted with a smile. 'I know him pretty well. You're barking up the wrong tree.'

She sighed and threw her hands in the air. 'Okay, fine.'

'Besides, they're all here for the rhinos,' Blake said. 'Not for donating to the community centre.'

'I know, it just came up in conversation what I do, and I wanted to take the chance to bring it up in case he or someone else might be interested, that's all,' she said. Blake could see anxiety written across her face when she spoke about the centre.

'Try not to think about work for tonight,' he said. 'Look at where you are, just enjoy it.'

She smiled. 'That certainly is the most wonderful

Christmas tree I've ever seen.' She nodded in the direction of the room's centrepiece, a towering tree – a real one – resplendent with white lights and silver decorations, topped off by a giant glittering star.

'What, you think that one is better than the one we did in the hall?' Blake said in mock-surprise, and she laughed.

'Well, I love the one we did,' she said. 'But it's not quite as impressive.'

He smiled at the memory of decorating the tree and realised it was one of the best Christmas-related memories he now possessed, thanks to Emily.

A waiter breezed past with a tray laden with Prosecco. Blake eyed it, remembering the crisp taste, and swallowed hard, fighting down the urge to grab a glass. 'Do you want to get some air?' he asked Emily, and she nodded.

'Follow me,' he said with a flash of an idea, 'And I'll show you something really special.'

✦ EMILY ✦

Emily walked through the ballroom, feeling dazzled and inadequate at the same time. This was a world she'd seen glimpses of when she was a dancer, but had never fully entered; the world of celebrity and wealth beyond imagination.

She was so glad that Tess had fixed her up with a gown and that she at least looked like she belonged, even if she didn't feel like it. Blake, for his part, seemed entirely comfortable in his surroundings, even a little bored by it all. She guessed that he had been to so many events like these – benefits, premiers, parties – that they no longer impressed him. He strode through the ballroom without so much as a glance around, whereas everywhere Emily looked something or someone caught her eye.

She was two steps behind him, trying to keep up, and she couldn't help admiring him in his tuxedo – the way it fitted him perfectly, like a custom-made designer suit should. His raven hair was slicked back, and she knew he drew the eye of all the single women in the room, old and young. And yet, to her surprise, she was the one who was walking with him out of the ballroom and into one of the lifts. She leaned against the mirrored walls and watched as he jabbed at one of the top buttons.

'We're going to the suite where my parents are staying,' he explained. 'It has a private terrace.'

'The penthouse?' Emily gasped.

'Sure,' Blake said, as if it were nothing, but Emily couldn't wait to see it. She knew she would never be able to stay in a penthouse suite herself, unless she won the lottery.

When they eventually got up there, the suite was more luxurious than she could have imagined. It even had its own butler – a serious-looking man standing patiently to attention, waiting to cater for the every whim of those who were staying there. Every piece of furniture, every decoration had been chosen with taste and comfort and style in mind, and she ran her hands across the back of one of the supple leather chairs as she drifted past. Blake led her through the French doors into the chill night air, and she gasped to see the dark green expanse of Hyde Park beneath them with the lights of the city sparkling like stars on the horizon.

'This is something else,' she murmured, walking to the edge of the terrace. She shivered as her fingers touched the freezing metal of the railing and the cold night wrapped itself around her.

'Here.' Blake removed his tux jacket, putting it around her shoulders. She grasped at it and smiled at him gratefully, trying not to feel too intoxicated by the scent of him drifting up from the fabric.

'What a wonderful view.' She sighed.

Blake grinned. 'It's great, isn't it? I've always loved how London looks at night. It's when it seems to really come alive.'

She nodded. 'Absolutely.' Her mind strayed to some of the wild evenings after work when she'd been dancing on the West End, and she pushed those intrusive memories away, aware of the danger of romanticising her past.

Strains of music filtered up to them from someone's open window – and she realised it was the sound of Bing Crosby singing 'White Christmas' drifting through the air, carried to them by the winter breeze. 'I love this song,' she said, smiling.

'Want to dance?' he asked, extending his hand to her.

She took it, feeling both foolish and exhilarated at the same time.

They swayed in time to the music, not really paying attention to the steps. Emily couldn't, not when Blake was focused on her so intently and she was held rapt by his stare. Their previous dances to the waltz, the tango and the salsa had been more studied, focusing on the correct movements and keeping to time. But tonight there was no structured dance with steps to follow and tempo to count. The only beat was that of her heart, the only audience the stars suspended in the vast expanse above them. They were just two people, swaying to their own rhythm; opposites drawn together like magnets, till the space between them was reduced to the merest millimetre. Emily didn't want to enjoy being so close to Blake, didn't want to feel the thrill of attraction that was surging in her, but she could barely breathe for how much she wanted to kiss him in that moment, despite herself and her better judgement.

She ripped her eyes away from his and looked out over the park.

'You're such a wonderful dancer,' Blake murmured, his voice close to her ear, the heat of his breath on her neck sending a shiver down her spine.

'Mmmmm,' she replied, not trusting herself to say anything.

'I was just thinking about all those awards and medals at your house,' he said.

She met his eyes, hoping he would drop the subject. 'They were from a long time ago.'

'Not that long ago.' He shook his head. 'Listen, I don't know what happened with your *Strictly* stint – I don't watch the show – but I do know lots of people in theatre, in film, in TV. I'm sure that I could get in touch with someone, see what opportunities might be available for you.' He smiled down at her benevolently.

She pulled back with a start at the unexpected, and unwelcome, turn of the conversation. 'Oh no, really, that's not necessary.'

'Don't be so proud,' Blake said dismissively. 'There's no shame in using contacts. It's a tough industry, I know that, but I'm sure you could still find work. Let me talk to the people I know, see who I can hook you up with.'

'No, Blake, you don't understand,' she said firmly,

irritated at how he wasn't listening to her. 'I don't want to. My dance career ended after that one series of *Strictly* ... I don't want to revive it.'

'But it looked as though it was really taking off. I just don't understand ...' He hesitated, frowning slightly at her snippy tone.

'What?'

'I just don't get why you gave it all up to work in the community centre. It doesn't make any sense.'

'It makes sense to me,' she said, her shoulders tightening with tension.

He shook his head in confusion. 'You've got all that talent, you clearly adore dancing, and yet you sit all day in a cold, run-down centre, worrying about reports and trying to make budgets work. You work all hours, you're stressed all the time, you have no life—'

'Excuse me?' she hissed, hurt at the casual dismissal of her work and his assessment of her life. 'I'm helping people who really need it.' Her heart burned within her at his words, the nugget of truth in them burying into her soul, stinging like a splinter under the skin. She knew she wasn't good at many aspects of the job, but she had chosen to dedicate her time to helping people, even if it gave her stress and worry and nightmares sometimes. 'Look, dancing is a passion, but it's a pipe dream. It was no good for me, no good for anyone around me.' She stuttered over her words a little, knowing she couldn't say what she really wanted to.

Blake frowned. 'If it's what you're meant to do then of course it's good for you. If you're just trying to live up to your family's expectations by doing what they do, you'll ultimately end up miserable and resentful.'

She dropped his hand, her eyes starting to sting with tears which she blinked away furiously. She couldn't expect him to understand her motivations, and she wasn't willing to explain them to him. Her reasons were private and would stay that way.

'You don't know anything about me,' she said quietly. 'Don't think that one visit to my house makes you an expert in working out why I've made the choices I have.'

'But I can see—' he started, but she held up a hand to cut him off.

'I should go,' she said, her voice trembling, crestfallen at having to end the evening so early when things had seemed so promising, but unable to countenance spending another minute raking over her reasons for dropping her dream career with a person whose ego seemed to deafen him to her protests.

He stared at her in bemused silence. 'Okay,' he said finally.

She turned and left the view behind, left Blake behind, and walked away, the night over, her passion well and truly extinguished. She brushed away tears in the lift. How could she ever expect someone like him to understand?

Chapter Thirteen

Blake tossed and turned all night, the luxury Egyptian cotton sheets bringing him no comfort or respite from the image of Emily's wounded expression that was now seared into his brain. He understood he had hurt her by bringing up her dancing career, but he didn't understand why that would be so painful for her to hear. He just thought he was stating the obvious, and surely other people must have said the same as him? After all, he *was* right.

He woke in the morning, feeling as though he had barely slept, guilt and frustration gnawing at him when he thought about how the previous night had gone. He hadn't expected Emily to look so beautiful, hadn't expected to want her as much as he did, and definitely hadn't expected to somehow aggravate her so badly that she'd turned and walked away from him and from the benefit.

He sighed and roused himself, showering and jumping in the car to go to the centre.

'Last day, huh?' Dan said over his shoulder.

Blake nodded, feeling gloomy. 'Yeah.'

'You look a bit tired, if you don't mind me saying,' Dan continued.

'I do mind,' Blake immediately snapped back, and instantly felt bad for taking that tone with his patient driver. 'Sorry, I just didn't sleep well.'

Dan nodded. 'Something on your mind?'

'Someone,' Blake said, and Dan nodded knowingly without saying another word.

Blake was simultaneously both glad and gut-wrenched that his community service was nearly over. He didn't feel like himself at all, and he knew that he needed to get back to normal life, to escape those people with their awful, sad stories that made him feel guilty for how much he had and how little they had. He didn't know how it was possible to both enjoy and hate an experience so much. He was comfortable with apathy, but the churn of emotions he was experiencing about this community service he definitely wasn't okay with, and he didn't even have alcohol to numb his feelings any more.

He got out of the car and took a deep breath before he entered the centre, shivering at how cold it was both inside and outside. He headed to the office and found Lizzie there on her own.

'Is Emily around?' he asked, both wanting and not wanting to see her, feeling torn and ragged by so many conflicting emotions and lack of sleep.

She shook her head. 'She phoned and said she was running slightly late today.'

Blake nodded and then he felt the door behind him open and bump his legs.

'Oh, sorry!' a voice exclaimed, and he swung round to see a woman dressed in pristine workout clothes, with her blonde hair in a neat bun.

'Hi, Tess,' Lizzie said. 'Emily isn't here at the moment.'

'That's okay. I said I would just drop something off for her today,' Tess said. She popped a plastic bag onto Emily's desk and turned to leave, looking at Blake properly for the first time.

'Oh,' she said, her face reddening, a sheepish smile spreading across her lips. 'Hi, you're Blake!'

'I am,' Blake said, following her as she walked into the entrance hall.

'I'm Tess, Emily's friend.' She extended a hand, wide-eyed.

'Nice to meet you, Tess,' he said politely.

'Emily said you've been doing great work here.'

Blake grinned. 'I doubt she said that.' He chuckled, and Tess giggled. 'So, Tess, what do you do? Do you work for a charity too?' he asked.

'Oh no, I'm a dancer,' she said. 'I'm currently doing *Chicago*.'

Blake raised his eyebrows. 'Impressive. Did you and Emily meet through dancing? I understand she used to dance herself.'

'Yeah!' Tess nodded enthusiastically. 'We met at Saturday dance classes when we were ten years old, and we've been friends ever since.'

'How wonderful that you've managed to break into the West End,' he said smoothly. 'It's a tough thing to do.'

She nodded. 'It's hard all right, very competitive.'

'It's a shame Emily didn't carry on with *Strictly*,' Blake said cautiously. His curiosity was sparked by last night's conversation, and he couldn't help wanting to know more. He knew Emily wouldn't tell him, but perhaps Tess could shed some light on Emily's reticence to speak about her prematurely-ended dancing career.

A shadow crossed Tess's face. 'Yes, well.' She bit her lip. 'After the accident, everything changed for Emily.'

Blake kept a neutral expression. 'Yes, that must have been tough,' he said. 'With the accident.'

'Awful stuff,' Tess said, shaking her head, her forehead creased with sadness. She checked her watch and sighed. 'Shoot, I really have to go. It was so nice to meet you, Blake,' she said with a slight breathlessness when she said his name.

He grinned at her. 'You too.'

She turned and left, and Blake watched her go thoughtfully, his mind turning over what she'd said. It sounded as though Emily had sustained a dance-related injury, perhaps a traumatic one, and decided not to carry on with her career. Blake shook his head. *What a waste of talent.*

He was distracted by Lizzie calling him, and he went to help prepare teas and coffees with Gloria and Fernando in the kitchen. He was kept busy at the drop-in, his last one, and he barely saw Emily. She drifted by, her instant coffee and clipboard in hand, sporting the usual intense expression she always wore at work. She glanced at him occasionally, but they didn't speak. The awkwardness of the previous evening lurked like an unopened rain cloud hovering above them.

When the volunteers had finished for the day and were drifting out, he hung back and went to her office. She looked up as he came in and quickly swiped her sleeve across her cheeks, where he was sure tears had moistened the skin.

'Anything the matter?' he asked, closing the door behind him.

'Oh, um, just some bad funding news,' she muttered. She looked utterly miserable. 'So, it's your last day,' she said, changing the topic with a weak smile. 'Congratulations.'

Blake coughed awkwardly. 'Thanks.'

There was a lot he could say, wanted to say, but he didn't know how. 'Listen, Emily, about last night—' he began.

'It's okay,' she said shortly, cutting him off. 'Thank you for inviting me to the benefit.'

'I just wanted to say that ... I'm sorry I pressed you about the dancing thing. Tess came in today and she told me about the accident, and I'm just sorry I made you feel uncomfortable,' he said.

Emily's head jerked up from where she had been looking down at her desk. She appeared absolutely horrified. 'Tess told you?! I can't believe she would do that,' she cried.

Blake held up his hands, alarmed at her reaction. 'Hey, I'm sorry. Maybe I shouldn't have mentioned it.'

Emily's lips trembled. 'That's private information. Very few people know what I did and I've worked so hard to make up for it, worked up from doing community service here like you, and oh! I'm so mad that she would tell you!' She grabbed a tissue and rubbed it over her eyes, where more tears were gathering.

Blake frowned in confusion at her words. 'Wait, what? What do you mean make up for it? What do you mean you were on community service here?'

She stared at him, her lips pressed together. 'Because of the accident. It was my fault. Didn't Tess tell you *that*?' She let out an exasperated sigh at his undoubtedly blank expression. 'What *did* she tell you?'

Blake squirmed, feeling uncomfortable at her distress. 'Only that you were in some kind of accident, that's all really.'

Emily stood up. 'Okay, well, good, because it's quite

frankly none of your business, Blake. Thank you for your time here. You can go,' she snapped. She brushed past him and walked to the kitchen.

He followed her, unwilling to let this be their final interaction. He grabbed her arm. 'Wait, Emily. I don't get it! This accident that ended your dance career, what happened? How was it your fault? Why were you on community service?'

She shook his arm off angrily. 'I told you, it's none of your business,' she hissed.

He scowled at her then, irritated by her unwillingness to let him in. 'You know, at least I'm upfront about the things I've done,' he said. 'I've never tried to cover up who I am, the bad decisions I've made, the problems I face. I never came here pretending to be anything other than a screw-up who made a mistake. I don't prance around pretending to be some amazing person who saves everyone else. I acknowledge my flaws, but you, Emily—' he jabbed a finger at her '—you pretend to be this charity superwoman, but underneath I think you're just as selfish and greedy and apathetic as the rest of us.'

Her mouth opened in shock at his words, and he knew he had said too much, said things he didn't even really mean, but he wanted to provoke her, wanted to see how hard he could push her, wanted her to open up to him.

'How dare you!' she said furiously, her fists clenched at her sides. 'You don't know the first thing about me!'

'So, tell me!' he barked back.

'You really want to know?!' she cried out. 'Fine!' She slammed down her glass of water, the liquid sploshing over the side. 'I loved dancing. It was everything to me. But it was also competitive, and so hard, and rejection was so frequent, and sometimes I just *knew* the girl who got the part was prettier or skinnier than me. I was so desperate to make it work that I was willing to try anything, take *anything*, to be the right girl for the part, to fit the mould.'

'Take anything ... like drugs you mean?' Blake murmured.

Emily nodded, blinking tears down her cheeks. 'Yes. Coke, mainly. It gave me energy but I didn't have to eat as much. The weight dropped off, and I got more offers. I thought I could handle it, but things got wilder. I did things I shouldn't have done. I took risks I shouldn't have taken.'

'And then?' Blake asked. Although he didn't want to see her in distress, he urged her to carry on, because he wanted to know her better, wanted to understand this complex, beautiful, talented woman who had come so unexpectedly into his life.

'And then I got the part to be a pro on *Strictly Dancing with Celebs*. I was paired with footballer, Kian Roberts. He really struggled and we were voted out first. I was gutted, as was he, and afterwards I had a night out with friends, trying to blow off some steam.' She shook her head. 'I don't know why I convinced myself and my friends that I was okay to drive that night – I was off my head. I should never have been behind the wheel. Tess tried to stop me, but I told her I was fine.' She took a breath, a shaking hand held to her mouth.

'You crashed?' Blake asked, though he already knew what the answer would be.

She nodded. 'I crashed into a roadside barrier. We were all hurt in some way, thankfully no one seriously or permanently. But ... the guilt.' She bent her head and sobbed. 'I couldn't bear it. The look on my parents' faces when they found out what I'd done, and the responsibility for hurting my friends. One missed a huge audition, and two of them never spoke to me again. Only Tess stood by me. Needless to say, *Strictly* didn't want me involved anymore, and there was some bad press. I swore that I would try to make up for what I did, try to make my parents proud, try to make amends ...'

'So, you came here on community service and ended up staying,' Blake finished for her.

'It was seven years ago, and I was only on TV for such a short time; no one really remembers now. I wish I could forget too, but what I did still haunts me.' She covered her face with her hands, trying to compose herself. He moved towards her, wanting to comfort her, feeling shocked at her revelation and guilty that he had forced her into it. She took a step back.

'Don't touch me!' she cried vehemently. 'It's all right for you. You are clearly okay with the mistakes you've made. Since you started here, you've not shown one shred of remorse for what you did. You only seem to care about yourself or what the papers report about you. You say that I'm just as selfish and greedy and apathetic as you, well, maybe, but at least I've shown contrition for what I've done and tried to make up for my mistakes in life. You, Blake Harris, you care for no one but yourself.'

Her words were like bullets and he stood and absorbed them, letting them sting him, knowing what she said was true.

'You should go, I want you to leave,' she said, looking exhausted. She turned away and refilled her glass of water, her back towards him. 'Goodbye, Blake.'

He looked at her, wanting to tell her so much more, wanting to change her opinion of him, but he knew she didn't want to hear it. He wouldn't be able to persuade her that his time there had changed him, that she had changed him. She was in no mood to listen.

He turned and walked away. His community service was done and he couldn't wait to leave.

✦ EMILY ✦

Emily listened to his footsteps, the sound growing fainter as Blake walked away. She heard the punch of the door button, the whine of the hinges, and the slam that indicated it was closed again. Blake had left the building, community service over.

She stood before the kitchen counter, clutching her glass of water, shoulders shaking with the effort of holding back her tears. She didn't want anyone coming in and finding her in a state; it wasn't professional. But the things he had said, and the things she had confessed, had led her to a tipping point where her emotional control was stretched to its limit.

Lizzie walked in behind her. 'I'm all done for today!' she called out cheerily, retrieving a left-over sandwich from the fridge.

'Okay, great,' Emily said, not turning around, her voice high and tight.

'See you tomorrow!' Lizzie headed off for the day, and Emily finally found herself alone. She turned around and walked back to the office, her vision blurred by tears, her shoulders sagging with despair.

This was not how she had pictured this day going.

First, there was the funding news, then Blake's almost cruel persistence in talking about her dancing career, turning the kitchen into a makeshift confessional that she had been forced into.

Emily slumped down onto her chair and glanced helplessly at the pile of papers before her. The voicemail was flashing, her email inbox was full. She had paperwork for Blake's probation to complete, preparations for Christmas Day to do, and a whole other host of work that, even if she worked solidly till midnight, she knew she wouldn't get done.

And she didn't want to. Not right now. Her motivation had left her, seemingly drained away with the tears that Blake had provoked. She sat and stared at it all for a moment, then gathered up her things, switched off the light, and left, locking up the centre behind her.

Right now, these things could wait. She needed to go and be with someone.

She paused outside the centre as she realised she didn't want to go and see Tess right now. She was still angry about her friend spilling one of her greatest secrets to Blake: the man who seemed to make her feel all the emotions it was possible to experience as a human being. Even River, whom she had liked quite a lot and who had hurt and frustrated her, even *he* hadn't made her feel the highs and lows of emotions that Blake had in just ten short days. What was it about him that turned her head into a riot of feelings?

Emily let out a frustrated sob and headed home. There was someone she knew would listen, someone she could always count on to be there and cheer her up.

Even if he was just a parrot.

Chapter Fourteen

Two weeks later – Christmas Day

✦ EMILY ✦

The streets were deserted as Emily hurried to the centre. It didn't surprise her that no one was out and about yet, it being 7 a.m. on Christmas Day. Everyone was probably still asleep, or perhaps waking up to a pile of presents to open with their families, or maybe cooking up a big breakfast. She pushed any encroaching sadness away. She refused to feel sorry for herself on Christmas Day when she had work to do.

She opened the door to the centre and hurried inside. She cranked up the heating and started preparing. She didn't like to ask any volunteers to come that early on Christmas Day so she was on her own to do the initial set-up, but she didn't mind. People would be here soon enough.

As she turned the ovens on in the kitchen, she tried not to think of her last conversation with Blake she'd had standing in that very spot. His words still haunted her, the sound of his footsteps walking away still echoed in her memory. She wished she wasn't so bothered by the way they'd left things, but she was. Blake Harris, for all her best efforts, had somehow gotten under her skin, and there he stayed, for now at least, like a splinter that had burrowed in deep, something she couldn't quite ignore. She hoped that he would be out of her system by New

Year's at the latest, but she felt a flicker of doubt that she could forget about him so soon.

By 10 a.m. the other volunteers were filtering in, and by noon the centre was ready to open for their Christmas lunch. The music was playing, the hall properly warmed by the heating being turned up for once. The delicious scent of turkey and stuffing filled the air, and Emily threw open the doors, delighted to see the crowd waiting outside.

She hurried around, forgetting about Blake and keen to make this the best Christmas lunch they had ever done. She occasionally took a moment to stop, breathe and take in the scene that she'd helped to create. Lonely older people pulled crackers with those who had no home. Ex-alcoholics shared jokes with Romanian immigrants who had no family to celebrate with. People in temporary accommodation came for a hot meal and made unexpected friends, bonding over roast potatoes and Christmas music. The hall held a multitude of people from all walks of life, and all their struggles were put aside this one brilliant, important day, to sit together in perfect harmony and pull a cracker, laugh at bad jokes and feel part of a family, even if just for a few hours. Emily knew *some* people (well, one in particular) thought Christmas was too commercial and tacky, but real Christmas spirit could be truly magical, and she felt that the hall was full of it today.

She bit her lip as she wondered whether or not any of this, any of them, would be here next year, with the funding difficulties they were facing. The thought was too awful to dwell on right now, and she pushed it away. She didn't want to linger on the negatives when the day was so full of joy.

Stuart came up to her while she was standing there and shook her hand. 'Merry Christmas,' he boomed. He looked like a different person; clean-shaven, trim, his eyes shining, a big smile on his face.

'Merry Christmas, Stuart,' Emily said, overjoyed to see him so well. 'How are things?'

'Wonderful. This is the best Christmas I could have hoped for,' he said. 'I bought my family today so we could stop by. Actually ... we were hoping to say thank you to Blake.' Stuart glanced around hopefully.

'I'm sorry, he's not here,' Emily said, wishing he hadn't mentioned Blake, which put him right back into her head just as she was beginning to forget about him for the moment.

'I thought it was a long shot,' Stuart said, shrugging, but still looking happy. 'We just can't thank him enough for what he did.'

'The job search went well then, I take it?' Emily asked.

'Oh yes, I've found a new role,' Stuart said. 'And apart from that, Blake's gift ...' Stuart trailed off, and Emily was surprised to see tears glimmering in his eyes. 'It's the kindest thing anyone has ever done for me.'

'What gift?' she asked.

Stuart blinked in surprise. 'He didn't tell you? He paid off our mortgage.'

Emily's mouth opened in shock. 'What?! Stuart, that's so wonderful to hear. What a lovely thing to do.'

He nodded and shook her hand again warmly. 'Thank you for everything you do here, Emily, and thank Blake for me if you ever get a chance to.'

She nodded, dumbfounded, as he moved away. She paused there for a moment, the generosity of what Blake had done for Stuart running through her mind. She didn't know whether to laugh or cry, but her thoughts were interrupted by Fernando calling her name from the kitchen. She hurried there to check on the food, assuring Fernando that everything was fine, and then bumped into Tony in the entrance hall. He stood tall, his skin glowing, his eyes bright. He had put on weight, brushed his hair and was wearing clean clothes.

Emily did a double-take to make sure it was him. 'Tony!' she exclaimed. 'How lovely to see you! Merry Christmas!'

Tony smiled at her. 'Merry Christmas, love. I thought I would pop by.'

'You're so welcome, come in!' she said, beckoning him to follow her to the hall, where she found him a seat. 'We haven't seen you for a couple of weeks. How have you been? You look so well.'

He smiled broadly. 'I've been in rehab. It's early days, but it's going really well.'

Emily grasped his arm, feeling a little overwhelmed by all the good news, a wave of happiness passing over her as she thought of all the years she had known Tony; she didn't think she'd ever seen him in such a good place.

'I'm so pleased for you,' she said, her voice raspy with emotion. She cleared her throat and sniffed, trying to remain professional and focused, when all she wanted to do was cry big, joyful tears.

He nodded. 'Don't go getting all emotional on me now,' he said, laughing at the expression on her face. 'But it's all thanks to the support I got here, and of course, to Blake.'

'What's he got to do with it?' Emily asked, bemused.

'He's my sobriety partner,' Tony explained, looking

surprised that she didn't know. 'And he arranged for me to go to rehab where he went. It's a brilliant place, the best. That man has pulled out all the stops for me.'

Emily nodded, unable to say more because of the lump that formed in her throat.

'Excuse me for a moment,' she whispered and walked off, taking a second to compose herself by the Christmas tree.

'Emily!' Rowan walked up to her, waving his phone. 'Can I get a photo of you standing by the tree?' he asked. 'You know, for social media.'

'Um, you know I don't like being photographed,' she said, clearing her throat.

Rowan frowned at her. 'Come on, Emily. I need photos of the community centre managers today. So, if you please?' He indicted to where she should stand and she shuffled awkwardly into place. Rowan looked witheringly at the tree.

'Um, who decorated this?' he asked, raising an eyebrow, and Emily couldn't help but smile as she remembered the afternoon she and Blake had spent working on it.

'Blake and I,' she said.

Rowan took the photo. 'Speaking of which, he's the hero of the hour, isn't he?'

She nodded. 'So I hear.'

'It's great about the money, isn't it?' Rowan said, absentmindedly thumbing through his phone to pick the best picture.

'Um, do you mean the sales from the decorations we made in the crafts session? I know, I was surprised we sold them all too, to be honest – but someone wanted the whole lot.' Emily took her paper hat off and fiddled with it. 'Although it's not really a lot of money, it's nice someone wanted to buy them all.'

'No, not *that* money.' Rowan looked at her like she hadn't heard him correctly. 'I was talking about Blake's donation. You know, to save the centre?'

Emily stared at him for a moment. 'The centre is saved?'

Rowan nodded. 'Yes, didn't you see my email? About Blake's donation?'

Emily had seen Rowan's email ping into her inbox, but when she'd seen the subject line was "Blake Harris" she had ignored it and decided to leave it till after Christmas.

She shook her head. 'I haven't read it yet.'

Rowan tutted under his breath. 'Well, Happy Christmas, Emily. Our financial woes are resolved.'

'You mean ...' she trailed off, barely daring to hope.

Rowan nodded. 'His donation will keep us going for a long time, help us to hire more staff, do up the hall, buy new equipment, fix the boiler.'

Emily took a sharp intake of breath and held it. Rowan smiled at the expression on her face. 'It's quite some news, isn't it? In fact, I thought we could get some really good publicity out of it too, but he didn't want any of that reported in the press. He said it didn't matter what the press thought. In fact, he got a little peeved when I asked about the media – he said that he wasn't just some vapid actor who was only looking for good headlines.' Rowan turned to walk away. 'Whatever he did here, I think it really made an impression on him,' he said over his shoulder.

Emily stood mute and amazed by the Christmas tree. Infused in all the joy of this day were Blake's good deeds, Blake's kindness, Blake's generosity. She wanted to forget about him but he was here, present in every piece of good news, his goodwill responsible for so many of the smiles she saw around her, and she couldn't help but run over and over in her mind the last thing she'd said to him and feel deeply ashamed that she had misjudged him so badly.

She stared at the tree lights, the ones Blake had unwound, and felt unable to shake the thought of him from her mind. It was only when she saw her friend walking up to her that she was able to snap out of her stunned silence.

'Tess! What are you doing here?' she exclaimed.

'Just passing by on my way to my parents,' Tess chirped brightly. 'I had to stop by and say Merry Christmas.' She wrapped her arms around Emily and gave her a warm hug.

Emily smiled wanly at her.

'Oh, are you okay?' Tess asked, looking at her with concern. 'Because you look really weird.'

'Thanks! And yes, I'm fine,' Emily said.

'You're not still mad at me for telling Blake about the accident, are you? Because I swear I thought he knew what I was talking about, and I may have been a bit flustered by his presence and let my mouth run away with me ...' Tess said earnestly.

Emily shook her head. 'Please don't worry. I'm not mad at you, honestly.' They had already talked about it on the phone, and Emily couldn't be angry at her friend for too long. She was, after all, the only one who'd stood by her after the accident, and she knew it was an innocent mistake that she'd blurted it out to Blake.

'So, have you heard from him?' Tess asked casually, studying her nails.

'Who?'

'Blake,' she said with a roll of her eyes. 'Who else?'

'Why would I hear from him?' Emily asked.

'I don't know, it's Christmas?' Tess shrugged.

'I don't expect him to get in touch, not after the way I spoke to him, without even knowing ...' Emily trailed off.

'Knowing what?'

'Oh Tess,' Emily whispered, her voice tight with unshed tears. 'I told him what I thought of him and I was totally wrong ... it turns out he's done really wonderful things, such generous things. I spoke so harshly to him, and now I can't even thank him for what he's done.'

'Of course you can thank him!' Tess exclaimed, turning the heads of people nearby. She lowered her voice. 'You know where he lives, don't you?'

Emily nodded. 'I guess I could go there ...' she trailed off again. 'It seems a bit intrusive though.'

'Don't be ridiculous,' Tess tutted at her. 'Go and tell him what you really want to say.' She studied her friend carefully. 'I know you Em, and I know he's gotten to you in some way. You should go and see him.'

Emily nodded. 'You're right. I'll go after Christmas.'

'No, go today,' Tess said, shaking her head.

'But it's Christmas Day! I can't just turn up!' Emily protested. 'He might be ...' She paused and remembered that Blake said he didn't have any plans to celebrate Christmas.

'He might be glad to see you,' Tess finished for her.

'I doubt it,' Emily muttered.

'I have to dash, but you better go today, Emily, or I swear I'll throttle you for your stubbornness.' Tess laughed and Emily waved goodbye as she hurried away.

She turned back to the task at hand, her mind reeling with possibilities. Should she go, or shouldn't she? In that moment she had no time to decide, as Darren came running up to her with a turkey-related emergency and she was forced to snap back into the management mindset.

For now, going to see Blake had to wait. Emily had Christmas to run.

✦ BLAKE ✦

Blake took a bite of his pizza and clicked aimlessly through the TV channels. He flicked past Christmas film after Christmas film, not wanting to see visions of happy families that he himself had never experienced nor had ever been able to emulate.

He wondered how Emily was doing at the centre that day. While he was physically here in his luxury home, surrounded by every comfort, his mind was firmly on the community centre. He thought about all of the people he had met, and he hoped they were having a nice Christmas, but most of all he thought about Emily. He knew she would probably be working hard, running about after everyone, and certainly too busy to give him a second thought. He doubted that she wanted to dwell on him at all in the past two weeks since he'd left, after their argument in the kitchen.

He regretted how their last exchange had gone. He kept wanting to call her, but every time his hand reached for his phone he stopped himself, remembering her words and her low opinion of him.

Blake looked around, and the only sound underneath the drone of the TV was an empty silence. Today, of all days, his house should have been filled with the murmur of excited voices, the sound of wrapping paper crinkling as it was ripped off much-wanted gifts, the clink of glasses raising a cheer, and the warming scents of stuffing and turkey. And for some reason, this year, his Christmas boycott was so much harder. *Maybe it was the lack of booze,* he reasoned, *or maybe it was the lack of family. Yes, that was it.* It was nothing to do with a certain dancer-shaped hole in his heart, he told himself.

He zoned out and watched a tedious documentary on the History Channel, numbing his mind with boredom rather than alcohol. As he sat in a melancholic fog, slumped on the sofa, the sharp sound of the buzzer to the gate broke into his thoughts, and he sat upright with a start.

He walked hurriedly to the front of the house, and as he did so, his heartbeat tapped out an anxious hope that maybe, just maybe, it wasn't carol singers, it wasn't a fan or just a delivery. Maybe it was *her*.

He clicked on the intercom and the screen displayed the face he had been hoping to see. Emily looked into the camera, shuffling her feet and biting her lip. She looked jittery and tense, but Blake could have punched the air in delight to see her there.

'Emily! Come in!' he exclaimed, immediately buzzing her in.

He swung open the front door and waited for her, feeling both thrilled and nervous at seeing her so unexpectedly at his home on Christmas Day. The frozen air immediately tumbled into the warmth of the house, but he didn't flinch. He felt remarkably hot all of a sudden; something to do with his heart pounding perhaps. Emily walked up the driveway towards him, her chin tucked into a large scarf and her hands deep in her pockets. The sky above her was a pale grey swathe of unbroken clouds, but they were backlit by a gentle amber glow – a sunset hidden behind a veil. The air shimmered with the promise of snow and indeed, as Emily reached him, he could see a few tiny white flakes falling from the heavens.

'Merry Christmas,' she said, looking a little pensive as she unwound her scarf and stepped inside. 'Sorry to barge in on you.'

'No, really, it's great that you're here,' Blake said, and he couldn't hide how pleased he was to see her. He knew he was grinning like an idiot, but he just couldn't believe she was here after how their last conversation had ended. 'Come in,' he said, beckoning her to follow him to one of the living rooms. Nerves and joy made him jumpy, and he hoped she couldn't see how his hands were shaking. He thrust them into his pockets.

'Oh!' she gasped as she walked in. 'Blake! Look what you did!'

He laughed as she spun round, taking in the myriad of mismatched tinsel and snowflakes and glitter and bunting strewn about the room, and the large, slightly lopsided Christmas tree that he had festooned with a multitude of decorations; a homage to the decorating style of the person standing before him now.

Having all those decorations in his living room had made his lonely Christmas more difficult to bear, but he was glad he had done it. It had made him feel closer to Emily somehow, forced her to the front of his mind, even though it would have been easier to shrug his shoulders and simply move on and forget his community service experience. He found that he didn't want to forget the centre and the things he had learned, and he certainly didn't want to forget her.

'It's beautiful!' she said, looking at him with delight.

'I thought you might like it,' he said, nodding at her approval.

She walked up to the tree and gently touched one of the baubles. 'These are all the decorations from the craft group,' she said in amazement. 'It was you who bought them all!'

He shrugged. 'Of course. I made at least three of them myself, and I wanted a souvenir of my time at the centre.'

Although decorating the tree by himself had been nowhere near as enjoyable as when he and Emily decorated the one at the hall, he had to admit there was a lot of satisfaction in using decorations that were made by people he knew. He knew the stories behind them, the hands that had made them, the challenges that had been overcome: like Bella's escape from domestic abuse, Linda's struggles as a single mum, Tony's fight against alcohol addiction, Johnny's mental health problems, Stuart's financial hardships. The strength behind the hands that had made the baubles, and the generosity of those who had helped, made those decorations beautiful, regardless of some misplaced glitter or wrinkled ribbon.

'Each of these has a story,' he said, 'and I wanted them here to help me to remember all the things I learned and all the people I met at the centre.'

Emily looked at him. 'That's wonderful,' she murmured.

There was a moment of silence where neither of them seemed to know what to say. Blake cleared his throat awkwardly.

'Um, do you want something to eat or drink?' he asked.

She shook her head and eyed the pizza box on the sofa with a raised eyebrow. 'Your Christmas dinner? That's not very festive,' she said with a smile.

'Well, it has turkey on it.' Blake grinned and she laughed.

Her face turned more serious as they sat down. 'Look, Blake. I wanted to come here to say thank you.'

'What for?'

'You know what for!' she said. 'Your donation for the centre. The things you've done for others. Things you never mentioned ...' she trailed off. 'Why didn't you tell me?'

Blake looked down at the floor. 'Well, you had a pretty low opinion of me and didn't really give me the chance in our last conversation.'

Emily reached out and took his arm. 'I'm sorry about what I said,' she said earnestly, looking up at him.

Blake shook his head. 'But you were right. I was selfish. And, to begin with, it *was* all about me, about what I could get out of it. But then I guess I realised how good it felt to help others without needing or demanding anything in return, the way you do it.'

She nodded. 'Well, you did help, and a lot of people by the sounds of it.' She paused. 'I'm so grateful for the donation for the centre. But more than that, I'm grateful for the way you were honest with me.'

He leaned back on the sofa and looked at her, giving her space to speak.

'You were right, about me,' she said. 'I wanted to come here to apologise for what I said to you, and to explain.'

'Go ahead,' he said, taking another bite of his pizza and

waiting expectantly, longing to hear what she had to say, hoping she could open up to him.

Emily took a breath as Blake chewed his pizza and waited for her to talk. She rarely discussed her past with anyone, but, oddly enough, she knew she could trust Blake.

'For years I've told myself that dancing was a selfish choice. That when I was a dancer, I made decisions that benefited only me. I was ambitious and reckless, and I ended up hurting people. Like, literally hurting them.' She paused, remembering the horror of that night, the smash of steel upon steel, the smell of acrid smoke burning the inside of her nostrils, the overwhelming fear that she had caused the death of her friends as they lay hurt and bleeding inside the crumpled metal of the car.

'I was so shocked by what happened that stopping drugs and changing my life was actually an easy decision at the time,' she explained. 'But that also meant stopping dancing. All I wanted to do was to make my family proud. I could see all the good they were achieving, and I felt like a huge failure in comparison. So, I started trying to be more like them. And when I was on community service at the centre, it felt better to throw myself into resolving other people's problems, rather than deal with my own. So, I stayed there as a volunteer, and then I got a job there and worked my way up to manager.'

Blake nodded at her to continue.

'I love my job,' she said. 'But you were right, Blake. My passion is dancing, and I miss it, sometimes I miss it so much that I have to take a breath and try to tell myself it doesn't hurt. I can't believe I made it onto *Strictly*, and although my partner was voted out first, I still could have done the tour, could have done more seasons. I gave up my career because I lost faith in myself and I lost sense of who I was, not because I lost my love for dancing.'

Blake leaned forwards and took both of her hands in his, the warmth of his skin making her tingle.

'It's not too late to try something different,' he said earnestly. 'You've done so much for the centre and that's a wonderful thing, Em – but maybe it's time you let yourself be happy again as opposed to trying to do something you think you're supposed to do rather than something you absolutely are meant to do.'

She nodded and didn't remove her hands from his, liking the way his skin felt against hers.

'I've actually booked in for some dance training,' she said, smiling.

'That's brilliant!' He looked delighted. 'Good for you.'

A shadow crossed her face. 'But I don't want to leave the centre and all the people I love there. I just want to find a way to dance *and* help people.'

Blake nodded enthusiastically. 'You could do that – there's no reason why you can't do both. The funding is all there for you, Emily. I assure you, anything you want to do, count on me. I have your back all the way. I believe in you.'

Emily was startled by his words, the sheer generosity of them took her breath away, and she couldn't reply for a few moments. Finally, she cleared her throat. 'Thank you,' she said in a hushed voice. She blinked hard, not wanting tears to fall, though they shimmered in her eyes.

'You're welcome,' Blake said softly.

'I've even booked a few weeks off in the New Year, although I have no idea what I'll do with the time.' She chuckled softly. 'Maybe I'll go on a holiday. I haven't had one for a very long time.'

Blake fell silent and looked at her thoughtfully. 'You know, I was wondering ...' He paused and cleared his throat. 'You remember my parents work with the rhino foundation?'

She nodded. 'Sure.'

'Well, do you want to go to Africa to visit the sanctuary? And then maybe go and see your family out there?' he asked.

She looked at him carefully for a moment, not quite sure what he was asking. 'That would be amazing,' she said slowly. 'Would you ... are you planning on going too?' she stuttered over her words awkwardly.

'Yeah,' he said.

'So, you're asking me to go on holiday with you?' she asked, a smile she couldn't repress playing on her lips.

'That's right. Go with me,' he said. 'You know how passionate I am about rhinos!' he protested in response to her laughter. 'And I would quite like to meet your impressive parents.'

'And then ...?' she asked, letting the question dangle in the air.

'And then we can come back, and you can do your dance training, and I will try to be a better person,' he said with a wry smile.

'I mean, are you planning to go back to LA or stay around here for a while?' she asked.

'That depends,' he said, leaning close and looking at her intently.

'On what?' she said, hardly able to breathe, her heart pounding hopefully.

'On what I have to stay around for.'

He reached out and stroked a strand of her hair, then let his fingers brush against her cheek. Just that one movement made her dizzy with desire, and she felt tiny sparks run through her skin and her cheeks flush where he had touched her. His gaze darkened as he looked at her, his eyes like a mysterious mist that she longed to become lost in. He drew one arm around her waist and leaned in close, running a hand over her hair and pulling her towards him so he could kiss her. She ran her fingers over the roughness of his stubble, breathed him in, delighted in the kiss, which deepened as she pressed into him. She raked her hands through his hair, something she'd imagined doing before, and pulled him closer. The feel of his hands on her sent shivers of pleasure flitting up and down her spine.

A small worried thought niggled in her mind that perhaps he was just acting, but there was a tenderness in his embrace, a look of genuine passion in his eyes, that just couldn't be faked. The man she was kissing wasn't the actor, the Hollywood star she had seen pouting with narrowed eyes on the big screen. This was the taciturn, moody, petulant unwilling volunteer who had turned out to be the most generous, the most supportive and the sexiest man she had ever met.

He drew back and rested his forehead upon hers, breathing heavily, clasping both of her hands together with his, entwining his fingers around hers and then raising them to his mouth and kissing them.

'What do you think?' he murmured. 'Would you like to be Mrs Harris number four?'

She laughed, knowing he was joking. 'Let's just see how Africa goes first,' she said.

They sat in silence for a moment, and Emily wanted to pinch herself to make sure she wasn't dreaming, that it wasn't all some kind of illusion brought on by too much brandy butter.

'Oh, and by the way, Emily, I forgot to say…'

She looked at him expectantly, thinking that there was nothing he could do or say to make the day any better.

'Merry Christmas,' he said, and his eyes were bright with emotion. 'And thank you, for the best Christmas I have ever had.'

'Merry Christmas, Blake,' she said, stroking his hair back from his forehead with a smile. She nestled into him and watched the Christmas lights sparkle on the tree; the tree he had decorated just the way she would have done.

Outside, the sky finally released the pending snow, the flakes swirling down, carpeting the ground in a mantle of white, and, curled up on the sofa, Emily realised that there was nowhere she would rather be for Christmas than there in Blake's arms.

Epilogue

'Jingle bells!' Emily sang happily as she flung multicoloured reams of tinsel over the tree. It was the biggest tree she had ever had for Christmas, towering over her at seven feet, taking pride of place in the living room. It was the same living room where, last year, she had turned up to apologise, with no expectations, to find the room strewn with decorations from the centre. Those same decorations were out in full merry force today; twinkling, misshapen, mismatched, and yet somehow completely perfect.

Blake walked in behind her. 'Good thing you never wanted to be a singer,' he said, mock wincing. 'You're tone deaf as well as tasteless.'

Emily laughed and turned to kiss him. He enveloped her in his warm embrace, nuzzling into her neck.

'Are you feeling prepared for the arrival of my crazy family?' she asked.

He grinned. 'I think so.'

'I can't believe they'll all be here this Christmas!' she said joyfully.

'And I can't believe you've left decorating the tree this late,' Blake said.

'I know!' Emily shook her head. 'I've been dying to do it sooner, but I've been so busy.'

Their home in Richmond was large enough to house the entire Williams family, who had decided it was time to reunite this Christmas. Emily was eagerly awaiting their arrival, which would start with her parents flying into Heathrow this afternoon, followed by her siblings into various airports at various times, but by 8 p.m. this Christmas Eve, they should all be here, and Emily couldn't wait. She had checked her watch about a hundred times already that day, urging the hours forward, and feeling as though time deliberately disobeyed and slowed down instead.

'Are you nearly ready to go?' he asked her.

'I don't know ... do you think it's ready? More tinsel?' she asked, stepping back and admiring the tree.

Blake chuckled as he stared at the overladen branches. 'Um, I think it's done.'

'Then yes, I'm ready,' Emily nodded and gathered her things, ready to visit the community centre before her family arrived.

She settled back into the car as Blake drove them and watched London slipping past. The radio pumped out Christmas hits, making even the traffic-choked streets seem like a merry excursion. Everywhere she looked there were Christmas lights, people doing last minute shopping, people hurrying to catch taxis, buses, trains and planes to be reunited with their families and friends.

As they walked into the centre, after Emily made sure Blake hadn't parked illegally, she noted with satisfaction the foil decorations hanging jauntily from the ceiling, and the twinkling fairy lights strewn around. The building was pleasantly toasty with heat from the efficient new boiler. It no longer felt cold and shabby and run down, and it had been given a face lift with new paint and flooring too. But behind the shiny new façade, the building still had the same old community spirit, and Emily felt it envelop her like the warm embrace of a long-time friend as she walked in.

'I can't believe my donation wasn't enough to pay for new Christmas decorations,' Blake muttered under his breath, and Emily pinched him on the arm.

'Those old ones don't need replacing,' she insisted, and he flashed her a sideways grin. She knew he was joking.

'Blake! Emily!' Lizzie called out, hurrying up to them with a delighted smile. 'We're just putting final preparations together for tomorrow's Christmas drop-in,' she said.

'Everything okay?' Emily asked, and a familiar old shadow of anxiety darkened her bright mood momentarily, but Lizzie waved a hand at her. 'Of course! Don't worry about it!' She laughed, and Emily admired her colleague and friend's ability to be so calm in the face of competing pressures. Lizzie managed the centre with aplomb and the clients loved her too.

She had hired Darren and Gloria and Fernando as assistants, and had a few other staff as well, thanks to Blake's donation.

'I'm just here to see the dance group for their final rehearsal before tomorrow's performance,' Emily explained.

'They're all in there already, I can't get rid of them!' Lizzie laughed, pointing towards the hall.

Emily practically skipped with delight towards the hall, tugging on Blake's hand.

They opened the doors and were greeted by the raucous sound of teenagers horsing around, exuberant shrieking and laughter, followed by a cheer as they saw Emily and Blake.

The eleven young people leapt up to greet them with wide smiles, eager hands outstretched and a torrent of excitable chatter.

Emily looked on fondly while Blake joked around with a few of the youngsters, remembering a time when he was desperate to leave this place. She never could have imagined he would be back here this year, by her side, his funds having paid for her dance programme for vulnerable and at-risk youth. Of course, she still taught the waltz to pensioners too, she thought, with a slight smile at his previous insult.

'Emily!' One of the older girls in the programme sidled up to her. Daniella flashed her a wide, brilliant grin. 'Guess what?'

'What?' Emily asked.

'I got an offer to study creative arts at uni!' Daniella exclaimed.

'No way!' Emily said, wrapping her arms around the girl, who a year ago came to them with a sullen face, a broken attitude and the threat of youth detention hanging over her. 'Well done, that's absolutely amazing news, Daniella. I'm so proud of you.' As the girl giggled and whirled away, a maelstrom of Charlie perfume, exuberance and bright pink lip gloss, Emily felt a gentle tap on her arm. She turned to find Jayden standing there, towering over her at six-foot, even though he was only seventeen. He shuffled his long limbs and gave her a sweet look from big dark eyes, which were bright with hope. 'I was wondering, Emily ... I er, I got an audition.' He spoke in a low voice, not wanting others to hear. 'Maybe you could help me prepare after Christmas?' he asked.

'Of course,' she said softly, delighted that Jayden had

an opportunity. He was one of the most talented young men she had ever met, his athleticism matched by perfect rhythm: two vital requirements to be a good dancer. But he also danced with such passion that he made the audience feel what he was feeling, and that was what made him a *great* dancer.

'Don't tell anyone, okay? I don't want to jinx it,' he said, and she nodded her promise. She had met many less talented people with bigger egos than Jayden, but he was growing up in a very difficult environment, with the threat of gang violence hanging over his head everywhere he went. She knew he was often afraid, though he didn't like to show it, and desperate to escape. This audition could be his chance to make something of himself, and she would spend hours helping him prepare if that's what was needed.

'I'll help you as much as I can,' she said, and she could see relief soften the nerves in his face.

'Thanks,' he said, sounding grateful.

Emily checked her watch. 'We better get on,' she murmured to herself. 'Come on!' she raised her voice and clapped her hands. 'Show me what you've got for the performance tomorrow, guys.'

The teens lined up in formation, ready to practise, and Blake returned to her side from where he had been talking to others across the hall.

'Did you hear that? Daniella off to university next year, and Jayden has an audition!' she whispered delightedly. 'Look what you've done here, Blake!'

He shook his head. 'No, look what *you've* done.' He turned to face her, hands on her shoulders, looking at her with the sincerity and honesty she knew she would always find in those steely eyes. He never acted with her. He was only ever genuine, only ever himself: her Blake, with all his many faults and myriad perfections.

'I am very proud of you,' he said and leaned in to kiss her, a beautiful breath-taking moment which was ruined by the squawking of some over-excited adolescents.

'Get a room!' they yelled, and Emily laughed, turning back to watch them practise.

She didn't think life could get any better than this.

✦ BLAKE ✦

Blake stood still for a moment in the doorway of the room, taking it all in, watching with amusement as Emily's niece and nephews grappled with their presents.

The air was filled with joyous sounds, the cheerful chatter of a family reunited, the rip of presents being unwrapped, the clink of glasses with a cheers to the season. The air was fragranced with the smell of mulled non-alcoholic wine, the tantalising scents of cinnamon, star anise and nutmeg lingering on their woolly Christmas jumpers that Emily had insisted they all wear.

His parents were in the Maldives, but he looked around and knew his family was here, because this was where Emily was. She was at the centre of the day, and at the centre of his heart. She was like a star he orbited around, and he was always drawn to her. Some people mistakenly thought *he* was the superstar in their relationship, but they were wrong. Emily's tenacity, kindness, talent and brilliance outshone him any day. He was just happy to bask in her glow.

His relationship with his parents was still difficult, but at least he understood one thing better about them now:

their all-encompassing love for each other. He had never felt that for anyone before, until now.

Being sober, settling down and helping charities had done wonders for his reputation, and he wasn't short of offers. But he had decided to forgo Hollywood for a while, so he could finally put some roots down and stay in one place – with Emily. He was in talks to do some stage acting in the West End, challenging himself as an actor, and for the first time in a long time, he was really looking forward to the next year and all the promises it held.

Rocky began whistling 'Lonely This Christmas', his piercing, somewhat pitchy, whistle doing no favours to the gentle, melancholic melody. He was promptly booed and told to sing something more jolly by Emily's dad, and the parrot began a manic version of 'We Wish You a Merry Christmas' instead, leading to a round of applause from the appreciative audience.

Emily walked up to Blake laughing, her curls loose and tumbling over her Christmas jumper. She looped an arm around him, her eyes shining with delight.

'Are you having fun?' she asked in a low voice.

'It's been the best Christmas Day ever,' he said, entirely honestly. Emily's family had gone with them that morning to visit the Christmas drop-in at the community centre. The dance group had performed to riotous applause, Emily's family had loved meeting everyone, and, best of all, Blake had the chance to catch up with Tony and Stuart. Seeing Tony sober and volunteering at the centre, and Stuart buzzing with plans for his new business, were the best Christmas gifts Blake could have hoped for.

'I just don't think things could get any better than this,' Emily said with a sigh.

He stroked back a curl from her shoulder. 'Really? You haven't got your present yet.'

She turned to face him, mouth open. 'Blake! We promised we weren't going to buy each other gifts! Now I feel bad!' She looked around frantically. 'Maybe I can make you something?'

Blake chuckled. 'Emily, you're a rubbish baker, and you make awful decorations. So, please, don't make me anything – really.'

Her face crumpled into a smile. 'Okay, but it better not be anything too special,' she said, wagging a finger at him.

'Oh, it's really not,' he said with a smirk, his fingers grazing the small velvet bag that nestled safely inside his jeans pocket, feeling the solid ring of platinum and emeralds that shimmered secretly in the dark folds of the fabric.

She smiled at him. 'Good. Now come and stand with us for a family photo.' She grabbed his hand and dragged him into the centre of the Williams' family scrum. As he stood shoulder to shoulder with her siblings and parents, squished together with the woman he loved, Blake had to tell himself that it wasn't just a dream. Because sometimes, well actually, quite often, he couldn't quite believe that he was part of a family, part of something bigger than himself, and most of all, truly, deeply happy. He had Emily to thank for that. He squeezed her hand and in unison they all chimed, shouted, squawked or yelled 'Merry Christmas!'

The result was a family photo of mismatched jumpers and wonky paper hats, some eyes closed and a few mouths open, no filters required, because it was full of Christmas spirit, perfectly imperfect, and there was nowhere else Blake would rather be.

Thank You

Dear reader,

Thank you so much for choosing to read *Strictly Christmas Spirit*. I hope it puts you in a festive mood and that you love Blake and Emily as much as I do.

This story is very close to my heart as so much of it is based on my own life experience. No, I'm not a dancer, and I've never been on *Strictly*, but I was a Community Centre Manager for the Salvation Army in London. Like Emily, I ran a drop-in lunch service and an arts and crafts session for people who were at risk, lonely, homeless or marginalised in the community. Like Emily, I too stayed overnight for a winter night shelter. And like Emily, I fretted and worried about funding and safety and staff too. I didn't meet a Hollywood superstar like Blake, but I did make some good friends, and the experience, while challenging, was extremely rewarding.

You may like to know that Rocky is real too, and can indeed sing opera! He is my friend's pet, and I was so happy to have the opportunity to include him in one of my books.

I love this story so much. Blake's turnaround, Emily's kindness and Rocky's humour truly have a place in my heart, and I hope they will find a place in yours too. If you've enjoyed *Strictly Christmas Spirit*, I'd be so grateful if you could leave a review on Goodreads or the website where you bought the book.

To find out more about me and for updates on my upcoming books, follow me on Twitter, Facebook or Instagram (details on the following 'About the Author' page). If you sign up to my newsletter, you'll get my free novellas to download as well as exclusive updates from me direct to your inbox.

Thanks again and feel free to get in touch – it would be lovely to hear from you!

Love Helen x

About the Author

Helen Buckley lives in Bedfordshire with her husband and two sons. After working in the charity sector in the UK and abroad, she turned her hand to writing and her first novel, *Star in the Shadows*, was published in 2019. She writes any moment that she can, enthralled by stories of fame, romance and happy ever afters.

Apart from being addicted to writing and enjoying soft play with her sons, she's an avid reader, action-movie fan and chocolate addict.

Follow Helen on social media to find out
more about her work or to get in touch:
www.twitter.com/HelenCBuckley
www.instagram.com/helencatherinebuckley/
www.facebook.com/Helenbuckleyauthor